The Journey of Sarah Levi-Bondi

R. P. TOISTER

Published by:
R. P. Toister
Miami, Florida

ISBN-13: 978-0-578-36946-4 (print) 978-0-578-36947-1 (ebook)

Edited by Carol Killman Rosenberg
www.carolkillmanrosenberg.com

Cover and interior by Gary A. Rosenberg
www.thebookcouple.com

Printed in the United States of America

In every child born . . . the potentiality
of the human race is born again.
—James Agee

It is so soon that I was done for,
I wonder what I was begun for!
—Epitaph for an infant in Cheltenham,
England, Churchyard (circa 1650)

Dedicated to all the innocent children who perished without knowing what they were begun for and to all the children living and yet born who can do something good for the world

For Brett, Kyle, Kara, Carly, Ryan, and Katie And especially Ellen for her encouragement during the writing of this novel

Prologue

SARAH LEVI-BONDI SAT ON A PURPLE COUCH in the antechamber of the Stockholm Concert Hall in Sweden on December 10, 1991, awaiting the announcement of her name as the recipient of the Nobel Prize in Medicine. She smiled inwardly and thought of the long journey she had been on since her birth in Rome, Italy, in August 1935. If fate had its way, she would have perished with her family in Auschwitz in October 1943. Her journey, and how she reached the United States and eventually arrived here in Stockholm, would have made a wonderful movie, but no film could have captured the drama of Sarah's life.

Sarah's blue eyes drifted to the large gold-framed door that opened to the auditorium where she would soon walk down the center aisle to receive her Nobel Prize from the king of Sweden and bow to the applause of hundreds. She looked at that door and began to drift in thought to a time long ago to another door that was not gilded in gold or opened to fame and awards.

Devi fare qualcosa di buono per il mondo.

"You must do something good for the world," her father had told her before her family was sent to Auschwitz in 1943. His words were chiseled into her memory like an epitaph on a granite tombstone. Her memory would be the only gravestone her family would ever have; they had all become black smoke drifting skyward from the chimneys at crematoria number III in Auschwitz-Birkenau in Poland.

1

On Friday morning, October 15, 1943, SS Ober-sturmbannführer Herbert Kappler entered his office, removed his cap, and sat on the black leather chair behind his desk. Kappler was a methodical man and looked to please his superiors in the SS. He had briefly spent time with the *einsatzgruppen,* or death squads, in Poland, so he had seen his share of murdered Jews. He had been a member of the Nazi party since 1931 and had risen in the ranks to a lieutenant colonel and was now chief of the Security Police and SS in Rome. Tomorrow, he would order the arrest and transport to Auschwitz of Jews living in the Rome ghetto and nearby neighborhoods.

On this morning, he summoned Captain Theodor Dannecker, his second in command, into his office and awaited his arrival. Their meeting was scheduled for 7 a.m., and Dannecker knew to be on time as Kappler had no patience for tardiness from his subordinate officers. Dannecker knocked on the door exactly at one minute to seven.

"Enter," Kappler said in a firm voice.

"Heil Hitler," Dannecker said as he entered.

"Heil. Please sit, Hauptsturmführer. I have reviewed your final plan for the Judenaktion tomorrow in the Jewish quarter, and with one exception, I will approve it. My one concern is many Jews might evade the roundup."

"Herr Obersturmbannführer, I assure you we will be able to round up at least one thousand Jews by midafternoon, and, while a few may elude the action, the majority will be arrested and taken to the waiting site for transport to Auschwitz," Dannecker responded.

"Do you have the information cards prepared?"

"Yes, here is a copy. It will be given to all families at exactly five a.m. when the soldiers are in place and the exit streets are all secured so few can leave."

Kappler held the card under his desk lamp and slowly read its contents. The printed card stated:

1. *You, your family, and other Jews in your household are being moved.*

2. *You must take with you:*
   A) *Food for at least eight days*

B) Ration cards

C) Identification cards

D) Drinking cups

3. You may take with you:

A) A small suitcase with personal effects and belongings, linen, blankets, etc.

B) Money and jewelry

4. Lock your apartment up—also the house. Take along the key.

5. The sick, even those gravely ill, cannot under any circumstances remain behind. There are hospitals in the camp.

6. Your family must be ready to leave twenty minutes after receipt of this card.

Kappler smiled. "Excellent, do you think twenty minutes is too long, and some Jews might try to hide or flee?"

"Some may try to hide, but there is no way to escape, as all exits from the ghetto and surrounding streets will be controlled and carefully monitored," replied Dannecker.

"Good, I am sure your plan will be carried out efficiently and on schedule. Remember, the action was directly ordered by Berlin, and our results will be evaluated and reported directly to Himmler," Kappler stated firmly.

"You already have the list of Jews and their addresses in the ghetto area, which I obtained from the Italian police. Also, remember, the Jewish community has paid fifty kilograms in gold as a ransom fee, so they are not expecting the action tomorrow," he added.

"It will be completed without any problems, sir," replied Dannecker. "Sir, I do have one question and a request. First, will there be any interference from the Vatican? Also, I am requesting one motorized battalion to assist in the action tomorrow."

Kappler slowly stood up and, after a short pause, stated, "The answer to your question is definitely not. I have been privately assured there may be a verbal protest for the record, but no direct interference will occur. In response to assigning a motorized battalion, I would prefer you asked for assistance from the Italian police."

"That is good," replied Dannecker. "It might have been a problem if there was any direct disapproval or protest in person from the Vatican. However, I do not totally trust the Italian police, so I must insist on a German motorized battalion."

Kappler paused before he responded. To any other

officer beneath his rank, he would have angrily repeated his refusal, but he knew Dannecker worked directly under Eichmann and therefore had a direct line to Hitler. He also was aware that he was Dannecker's superior in name only, so to refuse to supply the requested manpower for an action against Jews would greatly affect his own standing in Berlin. He ran his fingers through his hair, leaned over, placed both hands on his desk, and softly said, "Agreed, I will contact the SS garrison and instruct them to supply the needed troops for the roundup as you request."

Kappler saluted as Dannecker clicked his heels, returned the salute, turned, and left the room.

2

JEWS HAD LIVED IN ROME for over two thousand years dating back to 161 BCE. The word *ghetto* came from the Venetian word *ghet* for slag, a waste product of the iron factory near where Jews lived in medieval Rome. Since the thirteenth century, Jews had resided near the Tiber River until Pope Paul IV ordered them behind a wall in the year 1555 near the iron foundry, and since then, such walled-in areas were referred to as a ghetto.

There were approximately 12,000 Jews living in Rome in 1943 when Sarah's journey began. Most Jews lived in or near the ghetto area in small apartment buildings. Sarah's family resided at Via di Pescaria 18, a three-story building home to twelve families. Eleven of the families were Jewish, and the manager of the building, Pieatro Andolini, and his wife and daughter lived in apartment 1-1. Pieatro was Catholic and the nephew of the building's owner. The Andolinis had one child named Maria, who was ten years old and often played with Sarah. Over the years, Sarah and Maria had become close friends and would occasionally sleep over in each other's apartment.

On Friday afternoon, Sarah Levi-Bondi, a precocious eight-year-old, was waiting at her third-floor window watching for her mother and Mario, her five-year-old brother, to return from the corner market. Sarah spoke both Italian and English fluently. Her aunt, Ana Stein, her mother's sister, lived in New York City and was working at an international bank in Manhattan as well as teaching international finance at NYU. Aunt Ana and her husband, Saul, had visited the family in the summer of 1936, when Sarah was just a year old, two years before her brother, Mario, was born. They had given Sarah a cloth doll dressed in a red, white, and blue USA costume that Sarah had kept on her bed ever since.

Sarah was almost a clone of her mother. She was a very pretty girl with jet-black hair and sparkling blue eyes, and she often showed a mature sophistication in social situations. It could be said that, if some people were born good, Sarah would be the prime example.

She loved her family and looked after her younger brother in ways far beyond her years.

In Sarah's birth year, 1935, Mussolini sent 100,000 troops to invade Abyssinia (now Ethiopia) to expand Italy's territory. In 1943, when Sarah was eight years old, the Germans were in charge of Rome, and the Jews were in great peril. While she was only eight, Sarah's vocabulary in both Italian and English was more like an older child's and her ability to intuit others' emotions and sympathize with those less fortunate was the talk of the small community at her school and neighborhood. Her father was a pharmacist for one of the oldest pharmacies in Rome, having been in continuous operation since the 1800s. Her mother taught English in the local Jewish school. The family was not impoverished but had to budget monthly to pay for rent, food, clothes, and other essentials.

Since the German occupation, the fear was that her father would not be allowed to leave the ghetto area to continue working at his job. Rumors were constant about Jews being persecuted in other countries occupied by the Nazis, and chronic dread was the prevailing emotion in the community. Tonight, her mother would light the Sabbath candles, and on Saturday morning, the family would attend services at the synagogue. At least that is what little Sarah thought as she watched her mother and brother come into view beneath her window.

There would be no worshipping at the synagogue tomorrow, and Sarah would begin her long journey. None of these future events were even remotely apparent to Sarah when she opened the apartment door as her mother and brother climbed the stairs to the third-floor landing. When her mother reached the third floor, Sarah took one of the paper packages from her and walked into their apartment.

"Mama, did you remember to buy the sweet cookies Mario and I like so much?" she asked.

"Sorry, the grocer was all out of them, and he said sugar is becoming increasingly hard to get, so cookies may not be available for quite a while," her mother replied.

Sarah's brother made a sad face when he was reminded that his favorite treat was not in the grocer's bag.

Always sensitive to other's feelings, Sarah hugged him and said, "Mario, we can make our own dessert with some pasta and sweet tomato sauce, so let's be happy and not care about cookies tonight."

Mario looked at his older sister and hugged her

back and smiled, a smile that displayed his great love for Sarah and her way of making positives even out of disappointment. Sarah's mother smiled at both of her children and finished putting the grocery items in the cabinets.

"Mario, while I get the Sabbath dinner ready, why don't you and Sarah look at the picture book of America Aunt Ana sent you a few years ago? It shows wonderful pictures of New York City and the college where she teaches."

"Yes, let's get the book and look at it by the window while we wait for Papa to come home from work," Sarah said.

The children walked to the large window overlooking the street and picked up a large book from the table. They sat down on the floor and opened it. As Sarah turned the pages, she stopped at one point and stated, "Mario, look at the Empire State Building. It is the tallest in the world. Papa said someday we will all visit our aunt and uncle in New York City, and we will go to the top of this building."

"I would be scared," Mario said.

"No, you won't because we will be there together and I will hold your hand," Sarah replied.

"You promise?" asked Mario.

"Of course, I will always hold your hand when you are scared," she answered.

At that moment, the apartment door opened, and Sarah's father walked in, holding a large bouquet of flowers. Mr. Levi-Bondi was a handsome man with graying sideburns and soft brown eyes. He was wearing his white pharmacy jacket and a blue skullcap.

Sarah and Mario jumped up from the floor, ran to their father, and gave him hugs from both sides.

"Papa!" Sarah shouted. "You are home so early! Can we play cards before dinner?"

"Maybe, my *bambina*," he said.

"Honey," his wife said, somewhat surprised he was home from the pharmacy so early in the afternoon. Is everything all right at work?"

"Yes, I left early so we could start the Sabbath meal by sunset," he replied.

Her facial expression reflecting doubt about her husband's answer, Mrs. Levi-Bondi took the flowers and put them in a large vase, filled it with water from the sink, and placed the vase on the kitchen table. Then, after her husband kissed her, she took him by the arm and led him to the foyer out of earshot of the children, who were getting a deck of cards from the living room table.

"What is really going on?" she asked in an anxious tone.

Mr. Levi-Bondi sighed, then said, "Mr. Borchelli from the government bureau was at the store to pick up a prescription, and he took me aside and told me the Germans were planning some action against the Jews, and it would happen soon, perhaps even tomorrow on the Sabbath."

Sarah and Mario yelled from the living room for their father to play cards with them.

"I will, but first let Mamma and me talk, and then I will play with you both for a little while before dinner."

The adults walked into their bedroom for privacy. Mr. Levi-Bondi sat his wife on the bed and knelt before her. She held her hands tightly together on her lap, and her eyes were focused intently on her husband.

He took both of her hands in his and said, "Borchelli told me the Germans are planning to round up Jews in our area and deport them to resettlement camps. He said we should leave tonight or as soon as possible because no one will be spared."

"No, it isn't possible," his wife replied. "The pope and the Italians will not let that happen in Rome. The Jewish community raised a lot of gold to pay the Germans, and even the Vatican contributed to the ransom."

"The Italians and the Vatican know the Germans now occupy our entire country and have all the power. Do you think the Germans will keep their word and the Vatican doesn't fear being occupied by the Nazis? Don't be naive, my love, we have to make a decision now and not wait until it is too late. There are terrible rumors about the camps in the north and the east."

"If we leave, where will we go?" Mrs. Levi-Bondi asked.

"We can travel south and try to avoid the Germans in the countryside," her husband answered.

"No, we can't do that with the children. How will we eat or be sheltered? We can't live outdoors and survive."

"If Borchelli is right, we have no choice. We must decide tonight before it is too late. If the Germans come tomorrow, all the doors will be closed, and we will be at their mercy—and you and I know the Germans have no pity. *Il Tedeschi non hanno pieta.*"

"No, I cannot do that . . . what if Borchelli was wrong and we are alone in the countryside? No, we will be safer here with people we know, and even your manager will stand up for us with the Germans."

Mr. Levi-Bondi realized his wife would never be convinced. Even a home under threat was still her home. He slowly stood and, holding his wife's hands in his, helped her stand up. "My love, if you won't leave, let us think about how to save our children, at least Sarah, who is mature enough to understand if the worst happens. Please, I beg you to at least consider what we can do for her safety."

Mrs. Levi-Bondi, her head down, whispered, "Yes, we must do that. But if it is true, what can be done in so short a time?"

Mr. Levi-Bondi gently stroked his wife's hair and said, "I must tell you in the last few weeks I have been talking with the Andolinis, and they agreed to care for Sarah as their own child for a while if we have to leave or are taken by the Germans. Sarah and Maria are good friends, and they said they would tell the Germans, if asked, she is their niece staying with them from Florence. His uncle, who owns much property and this building, has friends in the government who will supply the papers for Sarah. We must take this action tonight. If there is no roundup tomorrow, we can make different plans. Mario will go with us, and when this nightmare is over, we can take Sarah back with us."

"What, are you insane? They are Catholic, and we will put them in danger if the truth is known. All in the building know the truth. It can never work. Besides,

Sarah will never go. She will stay with us," his wife replied with fear dripping from her every word.

Mr. Levi-Bondi put his arm around his wife's shoulder as she leaned her head against his chest. She began to weep quietly and murmured, "I know we must save the children, but why can't they take *both* children?"

"I asked, and Mr. Andolini said getting papers for one child would be difficult and cost a lot of money, and if his uncle asked for two sets of documents, informers in the government would become suspicious and might accuse him of collaborating with antigovernment factions. We must talk to Sarah before we put her to bed tonight and tell her what she must do if she is to survive. I know she will not want to stay alone with the Andolinis, but I will reassure her that we will come back when the Germans leave and be a family again.

"We must be strong together and encourage her as she has the best chance to survive. She is very smart and mature for her age. The Andolinis and her friend Maria care very much for Sarah and will protect her. If the worst happens, the Andolinis can eventually get her to your sister in New York. If Borchelli is correct, the roundup may happen very early tomorrow. We have very little time, so we must be prepared, my love. No one in the building would dare to speak out against

Andolini because his uncle is a powerful official with many friends in the government and can effect serious consequences for anyone who informs. After you put Mario to bed, we will talk to Sarah and explain what we must do, but she will make the final choice of whether to stay here with us or sleep at the Andolinis' apartment tonight."

They then sat down together on the edge of the bed until Sarah called again from the other room. They slowly stood and walked out of the bedroom with fear as their companion. They entered the living room where their children waited to play cards with their father, perhaps for the last time.

The Shabbat dinner was solemn, and when the dinner was completed and after they put Mario to bed, they took Sarah into the living room. Sarah sat on the couch, and her parents sat on either side with Mrs. Levi-Bondi holding Sarah's hand on her lap.

Sarah's father began by reminding her about the story of Moses in the Bible as an infant being sent in a basket on the river to survive. Mrs. Levi-Bondi then told Sarah that, at this time, they must do something like what happened in the Moses story since the Germans may start taking Jews and sending them away from Rome to camps.

Sarah said, "I don't know what you mean. What are you saying?"

"Sarah, we are asking you to sleep at the Andolinis tonight because I was told at work that the roundup of Jews in our neighborhood may begin tomorrow morning," her father explained.

"What? I do not want to stay with them. I want to be with my family," she protested and sobbed.

"Let me explain more before you refuse," her father replied. "You are the oldest, and the Andolinis can get you an identity card. The identity paper will say you are their niece from Florence, so you can stay with them until we return from the settlement camp the Germans have in the north. When we come back, we will all live in our apartment again as before. Mario is too young to understand what is happening, and the Andolinis can get only one set of identity papers. Also, Sarah you are smart and speak two languages, so you can understand what you must say if you are questioned. Please do what we are asking of you tonight, and if no roundup takes place, you will be back with us immediately. We would not want you to do this if we did not think it would be for your safety."

"I want to stay with my family. Why can't we all go to the camp together? I will be safe with all of you too," Sarah insisted.

Her parents looked at each other, and, blinking back tears, her mother said, "Sarah, you know we love you very much, and we would never ask you to do anything that would be bad for you. I know this is a frightening thing for you to do, but I also know you are brave and can understand that we feel this is for your protection at this difficult time. The Germans now control Rome, and all Jews are being threatened with being moved to camps in the north. If nothing happens, you will be back with us in a few days, but if there is a roundup tomorrow, you can stay with the Andolinis for a while until this nightmare is over, and we can all be back together again. We want you to do this, but you must make your choice soon so we can pack a small suitcase, and you can go down to the Andolinis apartment tonight. Please think carefully about why this is important now and know your father and I believe this to be best for you during this German threat for Jews in our city."

With his arm around Sarah, Mr. Levi-Bondi added, "Sarah, please listen to us. We know this is scary for you, but it is important for you to decide to stay with the Andolinis for a short while until the danger from the Germans is over for the Jews. You are very intelligent, Sarah, and I know someday, when you are grown up, you will do something good for the world. *Devi fare qualcosa di buono per il mondo.*"

With misty eyes, Sarah hugged her parents tightly and said, "I have to think about this so please give me a little while to make that choice."

"Of course," her parents responded in unison.

"Why don't you go to your room and think about this for a little while, and then let us know what you decide," her father suggested. "We will wait in the kitchen while you decide, but no matter what you choose to do tonight, please know we love you and always will."

Sarah grabbed her parents, hugging them both once more, and then walked slowly to her bedroom. Confused and sad, she sat on her bed and hugged the cloth doll given to her by her aunt Ana when she was an infant.

She thought, *I want to stay with my parents and Mario. What if I never see my family again if the Germans take them away? But if the Germans come tomorrow, they say I will be safe with the Andolinis and someday we will be together again. Please, Hashem, help me decide what to do,* she silently prayed.

3

On March 6, 1961, Sarah awakened to the alarm at 5:30 a.m. in her aunt and uncle's guest bedroom in New York. Now age twenty-six, she was enrolled at Rockefeller University and was to receive her MD–PhD in medicine in June. Her aunt Ana and uncle Saul had one child, Deborah, two years younger than Sarah.

Deborah loved her cousin, Sarah, as the sister she never had by birth. Deborah had received degrees in sociology and political science from CCNY and was enrolled at Brandeis University finishing her master's degree. She was an outgoing woman who was very attractive with long brown hair and looked like the actress Ingrid Bergman. She was active in the New York City agency for minority programs.

Ana Stein, Sarah's mother's sister, was, along with Debbie, her only living biological relative after the Holocaust and the Italian roundup in October 1943.

The Stein family was active in New York politics, and her uncle Saul was a judge in the Manhattan court system. Ana was a vice president in the international banking division at Goldman Sachs Bank as well as a lecturer in finance at New York University.

Sarah graduated from CCNY with an undergraduate degree in biology in three years and was accepted into the MD–PhD program at Rockefeller University with a full stipend as she had graduated first in her class. Her supervising professor was Dr. Samuel Goldstein, an expert in diseases, serology, and especially childhood blood disorders, including leukemia. He viewed Sarah as one of his brightest students in many years. She viewed him as a father figure, and as he spoke several languages, including Italian, they would often converse in Sarah's first language in the lab.

As did all new students, Sarah studied the history of this esteemed research center. She learned that, in 1901, John D. Rockefeller's grandson succumbed to scarlet fever, a tragic event, which motivated Rockefeller to establish a research center with the goal of biomedical research to investigate illnesses such as tuberculosis, typhoid, scarlet fever, and other disease threats to humans. Initially, the center issued research grants to scientists but eventually established a hospital and university dedicated to in-house biomedical research and treatment.

Since its inception, Rockefeller University became known as one of the most prestigious centers for research and education in the medical sciences. Admittance to the program was extremely competitive, and being accepted to the MD–PhD training program was considered a singular accomplishment for any student. Sarah was gratified that she was admitted in her first application as she knew many of the faculty were leaders in their field and had won many awards in science, including Nobel Prizes.

Sarah had arrived in New York in 1946, three years after her family had been gassed in Auschwitz, just one family of the 1,015 Italians on the train from Rome. Only eleven Italians on the transport survived the war, since the majority were sent to the gas chambers on arrival. The eleven survivors were chosen as slave workers and managed to survive until liberation in 1945.

She and her cousin, Debbie, had attended P.S. 14 high school in Manhattan, and both were top students and graduated number one in their respective graduating classes. Debbie was engaged to Alex Cohen, a fourth-year graduate student in the psychology program at Princeton. He, like Sarah, had many of his relatives perish in the Holocaust.

Although Sarah had dated in college, she never had a serious relationship. Always anxious about loss, Sarah protected her feelings in an effort to never be hurt, or at least that's how her aunt and cousin saw it. It was as if she constantly saw catastrophe on the horizon of her life, which was the result of the lingering effect of the loss of her parents and little brother. For Sarah, her mission in life was to try to fulfill her father's message "to do something good for the world." Becoming a research medical scientist was the path to that goal because it would allow her to save lives by helping to cure diseases, which, like the Holocaust, had taken thousands of lives, including the lives of innocent children.

4

AT 7 A.M., SARAH ENTERED Dr. Goldstein's lab and turned on the lights, as she was always the first to arrive. Her first seminar was at 1 p.m., and she wanted to set up the ongoing experiments for the week's work. Her duties included setting up the daily research schedule on the chalkboard, arranging the various chemical and biological experiments by area and researcher, and providing recent research summaries and references from the science journals related to the ongoing projects in the lab. Sarah was recognized for her reliability, thoroughness, and organizational skills in all these tasks. She usually completed these responsibilities by 9 a.m. when the other research assistants arrived.

Dr. Goldstein, while continuing to supervise the ongoing research, had many administrative duties, including meeting with donors to raise funds and to write grants to federal agencies to obtain project financial support. For these reasons, he often came into the lab after lunch and entrusted Sarah with the day-to-day lab operations and data collection. He was always involved in the interpretation of data and planning research directions but, again, relied on Sarah's advice and suggestions in both areas. Because of this, he and Sarah often had to stay for long hours after the daily work was done and came to admire, respect, and care for each other as a parent and daughter.

Dr. Goldstein was aware of Sarah's history as a child of the Holocaust, and because he had lost relatives in the war, he felt very protective of her emotionally. He often used a fond nickname for her in Italian, *polpetto,* which meant "little potato," an affectionate expression for children in Italy. The ongoing projects in the lab were all related to finding a cure for childhood leukemia. Sarah had been working in Dr. Goldstein's lab since her second year in medical school and had repeatedly demonstrated her acute observational and intellectual skills in defining problems and helping set up strategies to pursue research goals. Currently, the research team was working on perfecting bone marrow transplants to attack acute leukemia in children.

Dr. Goldstein arrived in the lab at 12:15 p.m. and saw Sarah talking to another student and munching on a peanut butter sandwich in the back of the laboratory. He smiled and waved for her to come over.

Sarah nodded, excused herself, and walked over to Dr. Goldstein's desk, carrying a sheaf of folders summarizing results of a literature search she had typed up the day before.

"Hi, Sarah, I need to let you know we are going to have a visiting researcher for several months beginning next week. His name is Dr. Robert Levy, and he is working on techniques to draw and evaluate bone marrow blood cells for cultivation prior to transplantation. He is working at Hopkins and is a very bright young man who comes highly recommended from their lab. You may be familiar with some of his publications from your literature reviews."

"Yes, I have one of his papers in this folder," Sarah replied. "It will be exciting to meet him in person and have him join the team, even for a short time."

Dr. Goldstein smiled and said, "By the way, Sarah, he is single, and you know how I would like you to have more of a social life. Maybe you two could hit it off."

Sarah blushed, as she often did when she felt Dr. Goldstein was trying to play matchmaker.

"Well," she said jokingly, "if you let me take more

time off from my studies and lab duties, I might be interested."

"OK, *polpetto*, I get the message—stop pushing you to have a social life. Let me see that folder you are holding."

Sarah handed the folder to Dr. Goldstein and said, "The article on bone marrow harvesting and rejection is interesting and suggests new technique ideas so you may want to look at that paper first. By the way, the author will be here next week." She smiled and walked away.

Sarah's few dates in college had been enjoyable, but her dedication to her goal always got in the way of developing a more serious relationship with a man. She had liked the last guy she dated because he had a good sense of humor and was not as immature as other men who asked her out, but a serious commitment was not her reality at this time in her life. She often wondered if she was rationalizing her hesitancy to develop a serious relationship and the true reason was her fear of loss given her history. Her family's loss was always a thought away, and she knew it would forever influence her life. She had talked to her aunt, uncle, and cousin about survivor's guilt, but they reassured her that, as a child, she had no control about what her parents decided to do, and she could always honor their memory by living a good life and pursuing her goal of saving lives.

As she thought about these things, she found herself visualizing Robert Levy; she had seen pictures of him in professional journals and thought of him as quite handsome. He was five years older than she was and extremely well respected in the research community. He was also Jewish. She pushed these thoughts from her mind and left the lab for her seminar.

5

THE LEVI-BONDIS HAD BEEN ABLE to bring some challah and a jug of water from their home before being moved to the detention location to wait to board the train to the resettlement camp.

The two and one-half day wait at the Italian Military College had almost completely used up both the bread and water. One daily meal of soup was given to the group while they waited to be taken to the train for the journey to the camp. In the early morning of October 18, all the Jews were transported by truck to the Tiburtina railway station where they were put in twenty freight cars with about fifty to sixty people in each boxcar. The train from Rome to Auschwitz left from Tiburtina railway station at two in the afternoon on Monday the 18th of October 1943 with 1,015 men, women, and children on board.

The train had been traveling for about seven hours now, and Mario was being held by his father and was crying because he was hungry and thirsty. No matter how they tried to console him, he couldn't stop sobbing. Some other people in the boxcar began to urge Mario to stay quiet and go to sleep. Mr. Levi-Bondi asked them to please leave him alone, as the boy was very scared and hungry. The Levi-Bondis' small suitcase and other belongings they had taken from the list the Germans had distributed were with them, but they, as all the people on the train, were told the items would be placed in their barracks when they arrived at the resettlement camp.

"Please let me hold Mario for a while," Mrs. Levi-Bondi asked her husband.

"No, he is too heavy, and you will need your strength when we arrive at the camp. I can manage, so try to get some sleep or at least rest. I am sure we will have a stop soon, and they will give us some more water and food," he replied.

"No, I do not think they will give us food or water. Remember, the Germans have no pity," she answered.

6

Robert Levy had been working in the lab for three weeks now, and he and Sarah had developed more than a friendly relationship. She liked him the minute they met, and in two weeks, they were having lunch together daily and, on this night, their first "date" for dinner.

As she was getting dressed for the evening, Sarah felt extremely nervous. She slipped on her navy-blue skirt and listened while her aunt and cousin gave her advice.

"Sarah, please calm down," Debbie soothed. "You know he likes you, and this is just a dinner so you can get to know each other better."

"Yes, you look beautiful so how could he not like such a smart and attractive lady," her aunt chimed in.

"Please stop," Sarah pleaded, as she buttoned her white blouse. "You are making me even more nervous. My hair looks terrible, and this skirt and blouse make me look like I am a freshman in college."

Debbie said, "You are *acting* like a college freshman. Why are you so nervous?"

"I'm not sure, but I think I want him to like me so much I am afraid I will do something or say something dumb."

"My dear cousin, you have an MD degree and soon a PhD and are working in one of the most scientifically prestigious universities in the world and are in charge of the daily lab routine, and you think you are going to be seen as dumb?"

Sarah looked at her cousin and said, "Not dumb in science, but socially. I always feel awkward with men who show an interest in me. I hide these feelings by being comfortable in relating about intellectual matters like our research. Maybe I should call him and cancel dinner tonight," she added.

"Cancel! No way." Debbie protested. "Show some courage. What is the worst thing that could happen? He will like you?"

"OK, OK, don't get upset with me, I'll go," Sarah said.

7

Robert and Sarah were seated at a corner table in Luigi's restaurant in Little Italy. It was a small but cozy room noted for good food, a pleasant atmosphere with red-checkered tablecloths, dim lighting, good service, and most of all, for the friendliness of the staff. Robert had ordered Chianti and some fried mozzarella for an appetizer.

"Sarah," Robert began, "I learned from Dr. Goldstein that you don't get out much socially and spend much of your time in the lab or library research. Dedication or a bad experience dating?"

"Not a bad experience," Sarah replied. "It's just that I guess I am a little too dedicated to our work, and I feel very comfortable tackling research problems and finding solutions."

"Why such dedication? We all take our work seriously, but you know, all work and no play . . ."

Sarah looked in Robert's eyes and debated whether

to tell him about her family and what happened that fueled her intense dedication to do something good for the world in their memory. After a few seconds, she said, "Robert, can I be honest with you and tell you the real answer to your question without sounding dramatically boring?"

Robert, smiling, said, "Of course, Sarah. By the way, I don't think I could ever find you boring."

Sarah told him the story of her family in Rome, the Holocaust, and her promise to herself to fulfill her father's request by curing diseases in children.

Robert listened quietly and fell in love with Sarah at that moment. He only wanted to help her realize her dream and take the journey with her for better or worse. He reached across the table and put his hand over her hand. She looked into his eyes and saw what he was feeling, and Sarah became both frightened and excited. They looked at each other in silence until the waiter approached the table to take their entrée orders.

After dinner, the couple strolled north along Third Avenue and held hands, talking about their feelings, and Sarah seemed happy, but nervous. Her thoughts were conflicted. On the one hand, happiness about Robert and a possible future of marriage, children, and a life together, and on the other hand, she wanted nothing to interfere with her mission in life based on her father's request.

Could she have both? How could she be happy when so many had died in the Holocaust, including her brother and parents? Was this survivor's guilt or was the feeling reflecting an underlying choice she must make between Robert and her almost fanatical goal to fulfill her father's wish and be her family's legacy and honor their memory? They reached the intersection of 33rd Street and 3rd Avenue; one block away stood the Empire State Building.

Sarah glanced up at the structure, then turned to Robert and said, "My brother and I had a picture book of New York City. We would look at it and talk about someday going to the top of the Empire State Building. Now, I am the only one who can do that for him. When I do that, maybe after graduation, I know that in some way, he will be with me."

Robert turned to her and said, "Of course, I will go with you."

Sarah stared into his eyes and replied, "No, I have to do it by myself."

8

SARAH WAS DRESSED IN HER GRADUATION GOWN to receive her MD–PhD degree at Rockefeller Center at 1 p.m. She was the youngest graduate for both degrees in the history of the University. In the previous year, she had coauthored two papers on bone marrow transplants with Robert and one with Dr. Goldstein. Their research was paving the way for the clinical use of new techniques to help children with acute leukemia and related blood diseases. Even at her young age, she was becoming known by researchers in her field as a brilliant and dedicated scientist and clinician. Dr. Goldstein had offered her a position as an associate professor at the University and associate director of the research lab.

Robert was back at Hopkins, and he and Sarah, by her own wishes, had put a hold on their relationship, but they still cared very much for each other. During Robert's stay at the lab, they had developed several new approaches to improve bone marrow transplants for ill children. While Robert was creative in developing techniques, Sarah's conceptual skills greatly enhanced which procedures might succeed and which approaches would be less effective. In lab animals, they had developed a model of leukemia and also studied chemical interventions to supplement bone marrow transplants.

At this point, Sarah was one of the most knowledgeable in the field and was being recognized by her colleagues as an important researcher in childhood blood diseases.

9

WHILE SARAH WAS ADVANCING IN HER FIELD, she
and Debbie were also very active in politics and civil
rights. They had supported and campaigned for President John Kennedy, and both cousins were constantly
monitoring any neofascist groups or propaganda.

In August 1961, after Sarah's graduation and her
taking the role as laboratory associate director, she
read in the newspaper that George Lincoln Rockwell,
the leader of the American Nazi Party, was going to
speak in Manhattan. Rockwell was a former naval pilot
and served in World War II and the Korean War. In
the 1950s, he published a magazine for servicemen's
wives and began to espouse his views against racial
integration and communism. When he sold the magazine, he moved to San Diego and soon became a
strong supporter of Senator Joseph McCarthy. In the
spring of 1959, he founded the World Union of Free
Enterprise National Socialists (WUFENS), which he

renamed the American Nazi Party in December. His group often picketed civil rights rallies and held public outdoor meetings where he would give long anti-civil rights and anti-Jewish speeches.

The meeting Sarah had read about was to be held at Union Square Park on Labor Day in New York City.

10

WHILE SARAH WAS GENERALLY a reserved and somewhat shy person, her underlying anger would boil to the surface when confronting any semblance of fascism or Nazism. The loss of her family was always a painful splinter in the flesh of her psyche and, like pain, could often erupt into fierce anger in certain circumstances. Confronting George Lincoln Rockwell and his followers was such an event.

Located between 14th Street and 17th Street in Manhattan, Union Square Park is famous for an equestrian statue of George Washington presented in 1856. The park originally was surrounded by residential properties until the beginning of the twentieth century when companies began to locate near the property. Tiffany & Company moved to the area of the park in 1905 and was followed by several other businesses, hotels, and apartment buildings. Historically, the park often was the location for political rallies, demonstrations, protests, and other events, including socialist and labor union celebrations. The park's name, however, was derived from its location as the "union" of Broadway and Eastern Post Road.

George Lincoln Rockwell purposely chose this site for his Labor Day rally because of its historic significance and location, and, in his words, "in the city controlled by Jews."

When Sarah read these words, her anger exploded. She even called Robert in Baltimore and urged him to travel to New York to attend the protest with her and Debbie while Rockwell attempted to speak. Robert agreed and said he would arrive the night before and go with Sarah and her cousin to the park on Labor Day.

11

THE TRAIN WAS NOW ABOUT 550 miles from Auschwitz. They had made one stop for water and a loaf of bread for each railway car and to change the latrine buckets. By now, everyone was exhausted and increasingly fearful, but most were too weak to even complain.

Sarah's family was now slumped against the far wall of their boxcar. Little Mario was so weak he often drifted into semiconsciousness, requiring his father to rub his face and hands to wake him up. Mrs. Levi-Bondi leaned against her husband and was now too weak to even shed tears. The odor in the car was putrid with a mix of urine, vomit, and fecal matter.

12

ON LABOR DAY, SEPTEMBER 4, 1961, Sarah and Debbie met Robert in Union Square Park two hours before Rockwell's scheduled rally. The park was already filled with reporters, demonstrators, and police barricades, as well as a large contingent of about thirty police officers. A group of Rockwell supporters were cordoned off to the right of the lectern podium. Sarah guessed there were about 75 to 100 of his supporters with some dressed in brown shirts and wearing American Nazi armbands.

Sarah looked at Debbie and Robert with an expression of anger and fear. She put her arm around Robert's waist, and he noticed her anxiety and discomfort.

"Sarah, have courage. We are here to show the world what this gang of bigots stand for will not be tolerated in America," Robert whispered in her ear.

Sarah held on to Robert and said, "The world forgets and moves on; only the victims and their families still bear the permanent scars of remembrance. There will always be hatred and violence in the world, even in America."

Debbie, never the shy one, yelled, "Today, we and others take a stand against bigotry and hate! By being here and shouting him down, we make a statement to the world and speak for the millions who can never speak again!"

The trio moved slowly through the crowd to get as close to the stage as possible, which was about fifty feet behind the front barricade. Behind them, there was loud shouting at a small group of Rockwell supporters pushing and shoving their way toward the podium. Several police officers flanked the group, trying to prevent physical confrontations with the large anti-Rockwell crowd on either side.

As this small group got close to Sarah, Debbie, and Robert, one large Nazi wearing a black swastika armband brushed by Sarah and said, "You look like a Jew bitch with blue eyes, and when we take over, you will be meat for the ovens."

Sarah lurched into Robert's arms with tears running down her cheeks. Robert shoved the man away and held Sarah tightly in his arms. As the Nazi walked away toward the podium, he turned and yelled at Robert, "I will remember you, and I'll see you later, asshole!"

Rockwell appeared at exactly 1 p.m. surrounded by a squad of eight neo-Nazis. He was quickly ushered to the podium, and when the crowd saw him, pandemonium arose. Screams of "Fascist pig!" "Nazi bastard!" and "Nazi scum!" filled the air. Many in the crowd threw eggs at him, while others tossed bottles and soda cans toward the stage. The police immediately began to pull anyone throwing objects away from the group of protestors toward parked vans.

A police captain, on a bullhorn, shouted that if any more violent actions were observed, the crowd would be escorted from the square. He added that while people may hate what the speaker stands for, by law he has the right to speak. The crowd began to "boo" and shout at the police captain, and it was at this moment that Rockwell began his speech, amplified by a loudspeaker system both in front of and to each side of the podium.

Rockwell spoke loudly and forcefully into the microphone: "Ladies and gentlemen, in America, everyone has the right to free speech, and when I am done, you can ask me any questions you want, but I assure you will have new information about our movement and that information will make you understand why we are going to save our country from Negroes, communists, and Jews."

Yelling and cursing, the crowd began to push forward.

Rockwell firmly and coolly continued, "In 1920, Winston Churchill wrote that communism was created by Jews, including Karl Marx and Trotsky, whose real name was Lev Davidovich Bronstein, a Jew, and so Russia was captured by Jews. So, you can try to shout me down, but you cannot shout the historical facts down. That's why Hitler tried to save the world from Jewish communism. He understood what had to be done, and he had the courage to do it. Our party will save America from Jews and communism and the Negro race, all of which are dragging our country into filth and mud by undermining our morals and principles like the queer Jew Gertrude Stein."

At that point, about ten men just in front of Sarah, Robert, and Debbie began throwing eggs and yelling and rushed the barricade and police line in front of the podium. Seeing this, Rockwell ordered his brown-shirted troopers to protect him as he stepped back from the microphone. Immediately, the troopers jumped from the stage, and a physical confrontation among the crowd, Rockwell's men, and the police broke out. Fists, bats, sticks, police batons, and tear gas enveloped the melee.

Several of Rockwell's guards broke through the crowd and ran toward the area where Sarah, Robert, and Debbie stood in shock and anger. One of the guards was the man Robert had pushed away from Sarah at the beginning of the rally. As he drew near to them, he recognized Robert and swung a large wooden stick at him, hitting Robert on the side of his head, which sent him sprawling. Sarah and Debbie fell over him, screaming and crying.

It took a long time for police reinforcements to clear the area and arrest members of the crowd and many of the brown shirts guarding Rockwell.

Rockwell had escaped in a limo parked behind the podium at the start of the violence.

13

ROBERT WAS ADMITTED TO THE HOSPITAL about an hour after the attack. Sarah and Debbie had ridden with him to the hospital and sat in the waiting room waiting for news of his condition.

Her face wet with tears and in shock, Sarah said, "Debbie, it is my fault. I should never have asked him to come to this hate rally. He only came because he loves me and wanted to support my hatred of the Nazis."

Debbie placed her hand over Sarah's and said, "Sarah, he joined us because he feels the same as we do, that hate and bigotry must be confronted early at every chance or eventually people will be hurt. He came because he wanted to, not just to support you and me. He knows the toxic effect of hate speech and how easily it can infect even people of goodwill. It happens all over the world and throughout history, and the result was that millions of children, mothers, and fathers have been murdered. Don't blame yourself for Robert's choice to do the right thing and stand against bigots. We both feel horrible that he and others were injured in the riot, but let us pray he will be OK."

Sarah nodded. "Yes, it happens all over the world and throughout history, but we are the *chosen* people. Chosen for hate, for rejection, for suffering, for ostracism, for jealousy, for blame, for scapegoating, and eventually for murder," she said.

Six hours later, Robert died as a consequence of a subdural hematoma. The cousins hugged and cried on each other's shoulders. Both women would never be the same.

Sarah never fully recovered from Robert's murder, and while over the years she outwardly told Debbie that she had come to grips with her guilt, inwardly she always blamed herself for his death. She often thought no matter what, the "Nazis" murdered everyone she loved. On the surface, she continued her work at the lab and interacted socially, but she secretly vowed never to fall in love or marry. Her "husband" would be her work to save ill children, and by so doing, she would continue to try to do something good for the world.

14

ON DECEMBER 1, 1955, a petite black woman refused to take a seat in the back of a city bus in Montgomery, Alabama. This act underlined the long civil rights struggle toward equal treatment under the constitution for African Americans. Eight years later, on August 28, 1963, Martin Luther King Jr. gave his speech in Washington, DC. The crowd numbered 250,000 people on a hot August day in front of the Lincoln Memorial.

Standing in the crowd were Sarah and Debbie. They had taken the New York to Washington train the previous day and checked into a small motel in Alexandria, Virginia. To Sarah, the civil rights movement was a symbol of the fight against discrimination and hate Jews had experienced over the centuries in so-called Christian countries. So, she and Debbie's traveling to Washington to support the movement for equal rights was both just and necessary as any minority could suffer even in America, the land of freedom and democracy.

Sarah knew Jews had been discriminated against throughout the years in America in college admission quotas, businesses, residential living areas, and even in joining certain clubs and sports facilities. Negroes, she knew, had suffered worse than Jews in America and also had the additional anchor of slavery to overcome and were therefore often seen as inferior by other Americans.

By attending the civil rights gathering, Sarah and Debbie felt part of trying to right the wrongs of generations and show the world the flame of fairness and equality still burned in America.

"You know, Debbie, if this were happening in Nazi Europe in the 1940s, all of the people here would be rounded up and either shot or sent to camps and murdered. This is why I feel so proud of Americans who stand up for minorities and the powerless."

"Yes," Debbie agreed. "I feel both hopeful and proud too, but realistically, I think there will always be one group versus another even in democracies. Jews in Israel fight the Arabs, Muslims fight Serbs, Protestants fight Catholics in Ireland, and on and on. Until there is one us, not us versus them, I fear this is the reality of human groups. Our only hope is to help minority groups to at least have equal opportunity without discrimination to succeed in any society."

Sarah looked at her cousin and took Debbie's hand in hers and said, "Deb, you are always so philosophical, but I think you may be right."

At that moment, Dr. Martin Luther King Jr. began to speak, "I have a dream . . ."

15

ON THE TRAIN JOURNEY BACK to New York, Sarah and Debbie sat beside each other as Debbie gazed out the window.

After some silence, Debbie turned to Sarah and said, "I have been thinking about King's speech and the way Negroes have been treated in our country. What if there were no Negroes in the United States and slavery had never happened? Would Jews have suffered more over the years than just being put on quotas to colleges, denied top executive jobs, not allowed in fancy rich clubs, and seen as inferior to the Christians in our country? King's dream may come true someday, but given the human condition of 'us versus them' throughout history, I doubt if true equality will ever be achieved by any minority group."

Sarah leaned her head back on the headrest and said, "I tend to agree that it may be human nature to compete with other groups, but in the United States, equality under the law should always be the goal of government. This includes voting rights, school deseg-regation, and equal opportunity for all no matter what religion or so-called race one belongs to. In Europe, Jews suffered for over a thousand years in pogroms, discrimination in school admission, jobs in govern-ment and science, social isolation, teaching positions, and social acceptance. Yet throughout all that, we still thrived in science, teaching, writing, and music when we were given an opportunity to compete with fair rules.

"But when things went bad economically, it was the Jews who were blamed and targeted in Germany and other European nations during World War II. At least in the United States, capitalism survived even though the U.S. had the same economic depression that gave rise to Nazism in Europe and the murder of Jews and millions of others. Negroes in the U.S. are discriminated against in all states but not chosen for mass extermination like what the Nazis did in the forties. That is why all caring people, like you and I, must always confront discrim-ination based on bigotry and hate. This is especially true in America where democracy depends on people speaking out against bigots and hate-mongers even if they are political leaders and officials."

Debbie reached over and gently turned Sarah's face toward her and said, "Sarah, I love you, but you are so idealistic. The biologically based struggle between groups will always exist and often depends on which 'tribe' one believes they belong to. Sports teams are a good example in all countries. Often rooting for your team against another team results in violence, either verbal or physical. That is why in the actual sport games, there are rules and penalties for violating those rules. The umpires or referees are in charge, and they are similar to the leaders of a country. If a referee is biased, then the game is unfair, and one team then has an advantage over the other. In a society, we call this discrimination.

"So, I do agree with you that which direction the conflict takes may always depend on a country's leader and/or politicians in charge. Principled men and women often do not become politicians. Even if they do, the system tends to be pragmatic and corrupt their motives either by money or coercion. What is the reward for a politician? Often, the reality for a politician is to be reelected and so to raise money for campaigns, they must compromise and/or water down any so-called idealistic social agenda. In the U.S., significant financial power is in the hands of the very rich and corporations, which usually act to advance their own agendas, and so they support elected officials who will endorse their interests. So, unfortunately, all it may take in democratic countries like the U.S. to foster discrimination and hate between groups would be to elect biased leaders."

Sarah looked into Debbie's eyes and replied, "Deb, you make me feel that there is little hope for humans to treat each other with respect and not to be prejudiced toward others who may be different from them. If this is true in America, then I feel my family died in vain and my father's request to do something good for the world is meaningless. I cannot accept that. I believe every time someone does something good for another person or stands up for the powerless, all humans take a step forward as a race, the human race, where we are all one. No, I will honor my father and my mother and my brother. In the next five or six years, we will be perfecting the techniques to transfer bone marrow for children with leukemia. Some of our research trajectories are based on Robert's work and combined with our lab data, has suggested new approaches to preventing tissue rejection, resulting in increased red blood cell production. If it is successful, we will treat all children during our trials for free without regard to their race, nationality, religion, or beliefs."

When Sarah uttered these words, she truly hoped that Debbie's pessimistic view would not be the guiding principle of her or her team's beliefs, but part of her feared that self-interest often conquered idealistic goals with human beings.

16

On Monday October 12, 1971, when Sarah opened her lab she found the official letter of approval from the National Institutes of Health funding the lab's procedures for a clinical trial on three children suffering from leukemia.

Sarah was now the lab director; Dr. Goldstein had left two years earlier to be the chairman of the medical school at the University of California. It had taken seven years to finally perfect the techniques for bone marrow transplantation without high rates of tissue rejection. Numerous animal and primate research with both successes and failures had occurred in the last seven years, and through it all, Sarah had steadfastly carried on, ignoring her social life. She directed the lab to pursue all positive leads and supervised the evaluation of all failures to discover where the research had gone wrong. She developed a reputation among her staff and colleagues as a brilliant and totally dedicated researcher, as if driven by some internal force of character.

After reading the approval letter, Sarah experienced mixed emotions. She felt joy at the prospect of finally putting all the research to use to help suffering children and sadness because the foundation of the research originated from Robert Levy's early ideas, and he would not be here to share in the joy if it was successful. The letter brought back thoughts of what could have been with Robert and the feeling of guilt that somehow his death was related to her and her cousin's fervent mission to challenge bigotry at every opportunity. As she sat at her desk rereading the approval letter, her mind drifted to visual images of her first date with Robert at the Italian restaurant and the powerful attraction for each other they both felt. As she visualized that time, she began to cry and had to leave her desk and wash her face in the bathroom.

I have to focus on the good that will come from our work, not the sadness from his death, she thought. "If we do something good for the world by saving the lives of children, it will give his dying meaning," she spoke out loud to the mirror on the bathroom wall.

Her father's request echoed in her mind and was the verbal rudder that always brought her back to reality and kept her focused on her life's mission. His words were the driving force that kept her working toward her goal even in the face of the painful tragedies in her life. She often wondered how a father's words to an eight-year-old could be so powerful and meaningful to her. She had read a lot about the psychology of survivor's guilt and remorse at having lost family in the Holocaust, but Sarah's feelings of guilt always evolved into anger and revulsion at the Nazis and others who created bigotry and hatred of other humans. No, for Sarah, at this point in her life, it was anger that was her driving motive, and, for her, to do something good for the world was a blow to the face of hatred and evil and the murder of helpless Jews.

17

It was October 20, 1943, and the Levi-Bondi family and the others in the boxcar were near total exhaustion. The train had stopped again for loaves of bread and some water but also had been sidetracked for several hours south of Graz, Austria. Almost no one spoke anymore, and two older individuals had died and were moved to the back of the boxcar. The smell was almost unbearable, but everyone was too weak to complain.

The Levi-Bondis were now huddled in the front corner of the boxcar and at least were on the opposite side from the dead couple. Sarah's father tried to keep their hopes alive by whispering that this horror would soon be over, and they would arrive at the resettlement camp where they could be fed and cleaned. Even as he whispered these words, he prayed silently that his family would all survive the journey. He silently questioned where God had gone. Why did the Nazis hate the Jews so much to inflict such terrible suffering? He had no answers.

The train was now about 450 miles from Auschwitz.

18

SARAH CALLED A MONDAY MORNING meeting of her team in the conference room adjacent to her office. The treatment team consisted of Sarah as director; Dr. Edward Nolan, an endocrinologist; Dr. Eve Grover, a specialist in hematology; Dr. Alan Tolman, a vascular surgeon; and three transplant nursing specialists: Steven Morgan, Ellen Travis, and Ben Heyman.

The group had been working together for over five years and had developed special techniques to harvest and transplant bone marrow in primates as well as special drugs to prevent tissue rejection in the bone marrow of patients. This would be their first attempt with a human child recipient, and the group was excited and somewhat apprehensive at the prospect of the first clinical trial of their procedures.

The first child in the approved clinical trial was a six-year-old boy from Baltimore, Maryland, named Marcus Williams. The fact that he was African

American did not enter into his selection for the trial since he matched a carefully designed protocol for the clinical study that included the child's age, no other health issues, normal birth and developmental history, leukemia diagnosis, previous treatments, and length of illness. Marcus was the only child of Rhonda and Curtis Williams. Mr. Williams worked as a carpenter in home construction, and Rhonda was an aide in a nursing home. Since Marcus's illness was diagnosed, Rhonda had quit her job to care for him at home.

The parents were interviewed, and a family history was completed as well as medical tests on both parents and Marcus to determine who might be a best bone marrow match. Of ten families that completed this evaluation, Marcus was chosen as the first patient to receive the transplant. Rockefeller University Hospital had designed a special sterile wing of four beds and an adjacent surgical suite to accommodate the treatment study. An additional apartment for the parents and family of any child in the treatment study was located in the adjacent office building/staff residence next to the hospital. All the evaluations and treatment were free to selected children and their families, and since the research grant did not support external costs, the University paid all travel and cost-of-living expenses for the family and child, including all follow-up visits and evaluations.

Sarah opened the team meeting by reviewing the Williams's family history and Marcus's medical and developmental history.

"As you all know," she began, "Marcus was diagnosed with acute onset leukemia when he was four years old, and after two years of treatment, his response was inconsistent with some improvement followed by a relapse. A bone marrow transplant was completed ten months ago, but his body rejected the transplant two months later. At this juncture, his treatment team petitioned our group to include Marcus in our research trial using our antirejection protocol in an attempt to save his life. All the data from our evaluation meets our protocol criterion so Marcus was selected as our first trial patient. After a complete medical evaluation, which will be completed by our team, Marcus's transplant will be scheduled as soon as a donor match is confirmed.

"We have data from several relatives and one in particular, his uncle Eddie, looks very promising. The final assessment on the match will be completed in two days. The family and his uncle will arrive from Baltimore this Thursday to confirm blood matching for the transplant. Therefore, I plan to do the procedure on

Monday morning, so please leave this weekend clear and plan to be in the hospital on Saturday afternoon to finalize scheduling if his uncle is approved as the donor on Friday."

The other team members nodded their approval, and Dr. Tolman stood and said, "We have been working for many years, and I know we have an excellent team and protocol. We now have a real chance to save young lives so I want all of us to remember that no matter what the result is, we will learn and continue to refine our treatment. I do feel our protocol will be effective and Marcus will be the first child to benefit and be free of leukemia. I looked at his uncle's preliminary blood match data, and I feel assured that on Monday we, and those who came before us in medicine, will take a major step toward curing this disease in children."

Sarah stood, smiled, and thanked the team for all their effort over the past five years and then adjourned the meeting.

19

After the meeting, Sarah sat in her office looking out of the window at the New York City skyline. She thought about what Monday might mean to her personally and to ill children in the world. She felt both anticipatory apprehension and happiness. Anxiety at the thought that the protocol would fail and Marcus would not survive, and happiness at the belief that the treatment would succeed and Marcus would be cured and live to grow into adulthood and, by so doing, pave the way for other children suffering from this illness to benefit from the team's treatment.

Her thoughts then drifted to her childhood in Rome and her father's message to her to do something good for the world. A sudden wave of sadness overtook her, and she stood up and closed the door to her office and began to cry. She missed her parents and her little brother, Mario, who she had once reassured that she would hold his hand when they visited the Empire

State Building in New York. She thought that soon she must visit that building even though she knew that her ambivalence about going alone, without Mario, had prevented this over the years.

Now, she could see that building from her office window, but the knowledge that her brother would never be able to visit it overwhelmed her, even at the point where she might help save other children from an early death.

Sarah walked slowly back to her chair and sat down in an empty office populated only by her sad feelings and her hope that the team's work would save the life of little Marcus.

20

On Monday at 6 a.m., the team met in the conference room adjacent to the operating suite where Marcus and his uncle were already being prepped for the transplant surgery. Sarah was reviewing the overall plan for the procedures and checking off the steps and role for each team member.

"Any questions?" she asked as she finished her checklist. "If there are none, then Dr. Tolman and I will prep for the procedures, which we expect to take about two hours."

Sarah and the team members rose from their seats and left the conference room.

At 7 a.m., she and Dr. Alan Tolman entered the surgical suite where Marcus and his uncle were prepped and asleep on the surgical beds.

Sarah looked at Alan and said a brief prayer out loud: "I pray we may do some good today and this child may benefit from our work and live a long life."

Alan nodded, as did the nurses at the sides of the two patients.

21

AT 10:30 A.M., THE PROCEDURES were complete and both patients were in the recovery suite. Sarah and Alan reviewed the procedures and dictated their notes into the recording equipment. They both agreed, from a medical standpoint, that the surgery and transplant had gone well, and the initial results would only be evident after eight weeks. The goal was to increase red blood cell production and reduce the leukemia cells and eventually Marcus would be cancer free as his bone marrow would produce only healthy blood cells. Much would depend on the antirejection protocol developed by the team in their years of research.

The medications to prevent tissue rejection were a key development of the team and essential to the successful long-term outcome of the bone marrow transplant. If the protocol worked, then the team would be permitted to try the procedures and medications on two more cases in the future. The next four-to-eight-week period would be one of careful observation and documentation by the team. Emotionally, all the team members, and especially Sarah, would be concerned but hopeful.

22

EIGHT WEEKS AFTER MARCUS'S SURGERY, his red blood cell count had risen to 11.3 grams per deciliter, only slightly below the normal level of 11.8 and was therefore in the normal range for African American males. The team was extremely happy with the results and were now prepared for the long-term monitoring and evaluation of Marcus when he was permitted to return home to Baltimore. He would be monitored at Johns Hopkins by a team working with the research protocol developed by Sarah's group.

On this day, eight weeks after the surgery, Sarah was going to present the up-to-date results to Mr. and Mrs. Williams and the written material for ongoing monitoring at the Johns Hopkins Hospital clinic. Sarah greeted them in the waiting room and accompanied them to her office. She took a seat behind her desk, and the Williamses sat on two chairs in front of her.

"Mr. and Mrs. Williams," Sarah began, "I know this has been a difficult eight weeks for you both and you have been patiently waiting for the first blood results. I am happy to inform you, given the blood work, Marcus's red blood cell count is now within normal limits. I have to tell you, however, while the indication is that the transplant and antirejection protocol seem to be working, we have to be cautiously optimistic. You both know from our intake and treatment discussions that Marcus is our first patient to be treated with our protocol, and so he will be followed at Hopkins on a monthly basis, but we feel that you will be able to take him home tomorrow."

Mrs. Williams began crying and rose to her feet and bent over to hug Sarah. "Oh, doctor, we thank you and your team from the bottom of our hearts. We know there is no guarantee for the long term, but Marcus looks so much better and seems so much healthier that we pray that the treatment will continue to work."

Mr. Williams stood up next to his wife and took out a handkerchief from his back pocket. He wiped away a tear. "I know that I could only visit on the weekends, but I see how much stronger and better Marcus is in the last four weeks. God bless you and your team for doing something so good for our small family. I will tell his uncle that his help was an important thing so far to help Marcus."

With a serious expression, Sarah said, "Mr. Williams, while we hope that the treatment is a cure, again I must remind you both that we still have at least one year to follow Marcus before we can be more certain that the problem will not return. The information so far is positive, but let us follow up before coming to a final conclusion about a permanent cure."

"We know," Mr. Williams replied, "but we have had little positive hope before, so this is the first real sign that Marcus has the possibility of living, and for that, we are thankful. We will faithfully stick to the monthly follow-up schedule at Hopkins and do whatever is required to keep Marcus on the right track. We will always be appreciative to you and your team. God bless you all."

Sarah stood, and she and Marcus's parents hugged for what seemed like a long time.

23

I᷈T WAS ONE YEAR AFTER the treatment of Marcus Williams, and he continued to show no signs of leukemia in his monthly evaluations at the Johns Hopkins clinic. The team was given approval for a second patient trial, and Sarah reviewed several patient applications. After reviewing many files, one little girl's file caught her attention.

The girl's name was Susan Abrams. She was eight years old and lived with her parents in Ossining, New York, about thirty miles north of New York City. What made Susan's case interesting to Sarah was her age and the fact that her disease had developed somewhat later in her life compared to other children with leukemia. If the team's treatment protocol could help older children, it would mean hope for both children with early and late onset of the disease.

Susan was seven years old when she was first diagnosed and did not respond to one year of treatment with chemical intervention. The medical team at Columbia University Medical Center in New York City had referred her. Another factor that made Susan's case interesting was that she had a fraternal twin brother who did not show any signs of the disease. However, he could be a good match for a bone marrow transplant if her parents or other relatives did not qualify.

The Abrams family was scheduled to be interviewed on Friday at the clinic, and preliminary blood work taken from Susan and her brother would be evaluated that weekend. The urgency was related to Susan's age and the circumstance that she was at greater risk due to the fact that she had not responded to treatment. Sarah had requested that the team work over the weekend because, if the results were promising and Susan's brother was a match for a transplant, the procedure would be scheduled for the following Wednesday. While this schedule was somewhat of a rush, Sarah and the team felt that given their experience with the procedures, they would not be jeopardizing the treatment outcome by compressing the treatment schedule.

On Friday, the Abrams family arrived at the hospital and were interviewed by Sarah and Dr. Tolman in the lab conference room. Ann Abrams was a petite woman with black hair and green eyes. She was obviously very nervous and sat next to Susan and held her arm around her daughter's shoulder. Her husband, David, was tall and thin with graying brown hair. He sat next to his wife with his son, Robert, at his side. Robert was a handsome boy who looked a great deal like his father. Susan was a clone of her mother with green eyes and dark hair, but much smaller in stature than her fraternal twin brother. She was obviously very ill and pale and seemed very anxious as she stared at Sarah and Dr. Tolman.

Sarah began, "We are very glad you all could make this appointment at such short notice, and please ask if you need anything to drink or have any questions about the treatment. Please do not hesitate to interrupt if you have a question or comment. While we have a lot of information to present and review, we would like to keep this meeting as informal as possible; our team views our treatment as a collaboration with your family."

Mrs. Abrams asked, "If Robert is a match and we decide to proceed, when could the procedure be done?"

Sarah replied, "If all goes well with the lab tests and there is a donor match, then we could schedule the procedure next week on Wednesday. However, this depends on many factors, including the team's assessment of all the information, the likelihood of success in the long run, and verbal approval of the National Institutes of Health, which funds and monitors our program."

Mr. Abrams looked at his son and asked, "What will the procedure mean for the donor?"

Dr. Tolman glanced at Sarah and then responded, "The procedure involves side-by-side surgery with both the donor and recipient under anesthesia and probably takes about two hours, with approximately a twenty-four-hour recovery in the unit before being transferred to the germ-free suite for the recipient."

Sarah placed her hand on Mrs. Abrams's arm and asked, "Is it OK if one of our nurses takes Robert and Susan to the playroom down the hall for a few minutes while we discuss the procedure in more detail?"

When the children left, Sarah turned to the Abramses and stated, "I know how difficult this is for you both, and you are probably anxious about any pain or discomfort for both of your children. While there will be some moderate pain during recovery for both, and some ongoing pain for Susan during post-surgery chemical treatment to ensure her immune system does not reject the bone marrow transplant, all efforts will be made to minimize the effects of the treatment discomfort. However, we must balance the possible benefit of a successful outcome for Susan against the distress of the treatment protocol."

Mr. and Mrs. Abrams looked at each other, and then Mr. Abrams hugged his wife as she began to sob. He then turned to Sarah and said, "We have seen Susan go through so much in the last year and wish we could take her pain away. We understand that without this intervention she has little hope of a cure or remission, so we will agree to the treatment."

Dr. Tolman looked at Sarah and then at the Abramses and said, "We understand how you feel, and we will always try to minimize her pain, but we agree that her best hope now is to be treated with a bone marrow transplant if all criteria are met. While we cannot guarantee Susan will respond and be in remission or cured, we know she has a good chance to respond in a positive way to the treatment. If we proceed, your family will become part of our team, and encouraging Susan will be an important part of the protocol. We need you both to understand how important this is and to be positive, especially when talking to her. We found this to be very helpful with our previous patient. So can you both agree to this approach?"

The couple looked at each other and, as Mrs. Abrams wiped tears from her eyes, both responded affirmatively with a nod.

24

EIGHT WEEKS AFTER THE SURGERY, Susan was responding very well, and her red blood cell count rose to almost normal levels. While it would take another ten months of monitoring to fulfill the protocol's guidelines, the team and the family were very optimistic. Susan would be on antirejection medication during that time, but she was tolerating the chemicals without any major side effects.

In the update conference with Susan's parents, Sarah escorted them into her office and sat down behind her desk. She began, "So far, as you can see, Susan is responding positively to the transplant and treatment. You both understand that our protocol calls for a ten-month follow-up with monthly visits and evaluations followed by visits every three months after that. So even though the initial results make us all optimistic, until then, we still have to be cautious in making any long-term predictions."

Susan's dad said, "We know and understand, but we want to thank you and the team for giving us hope and the possibility of a long-term cure for our daughter."

His wife added, "My husband and I were so worried about the suffering Susan would have to endure with the treatment that we were anxious, and I want to apologize for my negative attitude before the transplant. I also want to say that you and your team are so supportive and understanding that it has made us so much more comfortable and hopeful for Susan. All of you are really doing something good for sick children and their families."

Hearing that last comment, Sarah had a mental flashback of her father's words to do something good for the world. She almost became teary eyed but fought the urge and tried to remain professional in the presence of Mr. and Mrs. Abrams. It was Friday, December 1, 1974.

25

THAT EVENING SARAH WENT TO Debbie's apartment for dinner. Debbie and her husband, Alex Cohen, had gotten married in 1967 after he had graduated from Princeton University with a PhD in psychology. They had no children as Debbie was unable to conceive, which, while disappointing, had not negatively affected the marriage. Both Debbie and Alex were active in sponsoring a visiting college student from other countries, especially from Israel and Italy.

During the school year, the student lived on the Columbia University campus and every third Friday of the month attended a dinner at the Cohen apartment. After dinner, the group had interesting discussions about medicine, history, science, and human behavior. Sarah often participated in these monthly dinners, which included other scholars from a variety of fields, including law, economics, philosophy, science, and medicine.

On this Friday evening, those attending the dinner included Debbie and Alex; Anton Witkin, a renowned historian from Columbia University; Shaun Sullivan, the department head of Religious Studies at New York University; and Rosanna Moscati, the visiting student scholar from Italy.

After dinner, the small group gathered in the living room to have coffee, tea, and dessert and to talk about current topics in science, human development, the economy, and religion.

Debbie began the discussion by addressing Sarah, "I heard from you last week that the second trial of your team's treatment went well so far, is that correct?"

"Yes, if the results stay positive for another ten months, we can recruit a third patient, and if that is successful, our approach can be expanded to a larger group of children," Sarah replied.

Anton Witkin was a small, bald man with piercing brown eyes who was a distinguished professor of European history at Columbia University. His lectures were always packed with students, and he had published many books, including a major work on morality in European culture from the 1600s to the end of World War II. While his knowledge and intelligence were always impressive to both students and scholars, he was also feared as someone who spoke his mind—even if he came across as insensitive to others. Often his initial questioning of a colleague or student seemed innocuous but would be quickly followed by a challenge to the other person's point of view or beliefs. Tonight would be no different as he addressed Sarah about her treatment program.

"I know some information about your work from Debbie, but I wonder how you and your team select a child for treatment," asked Witkin.

Sarah responded by briefly summarizing the protocol and selection criteria for the historian.

"Yes, it seems to be a very thorough and well-thought-out process, but what if, given your personal history, a child was the grandson of a Nazi war criminal. Would that influence your team's decision to include that child in the treatment study?"

Visually shaken by this unexpected question, Sarah immediately replied, "No, from a medical and ethical point of view, we would only consider the health and needs of the child, regardless of family background or family issues."

"Then, for purposes of tonight's discussion, knowing your history and what happened to your family, I propose a hypothetical topic. Your team is approached by the parents of a child who is the grandson of a Nazi war criminal or even more relevant to you Sarah, Herbert Kappler or his deputy Theodor Dannecker, the men who ordered and carried out the roundup and deportation of the Jews in Rome in 1943, including your family," Witkin said.

There was an immediate stunned silence in the room, as the other guests looked at Witkin with surprise and disapproval, as if this topic was very inappropriate for the night's discussion given Sarah's history.

Aware of the changed atmosphere in the group, Witkin said, "I know that this topic may be very uncomfortable, but as a historian, I often see how emotion, not reason, influences a person's actions, so I think it is a very important issue for discussion by this group. I would add that your team's selection criteria are in direct contrast to the code that the physicians and leaders of the Third Reich used to justify their terrible acts. Therefore, if Sarah approves, we can discuss these moral and ethical issues in Germany compared to her group's moral and ethical code now."

Rosanna, the student from Italy, interrupted and, in a loud voice, said, "As an Italian Jew in current-day Italy, I have studied the German occupation during World War II. I do not think this topic has any relevance to what German leaders believed since it was their actions that defined murder, robbery, and exploitation of conquered countries. So, we can talk theoretically about the actions of the Germans historically and how it might now relate to Dr. Levi-Bondi professionally or personally, but to me, it seems to be a meaningless and somewhat rude topic for tonight's discussion."

Alex added, "As a psychologist, I tend to agree with Rosanna that we can only judge the Germans at that time in Italy by their actions. From a practical point of view, they committed murder, robbery, and conquered weaker nations by military force. However, as to the question about whether Sarah's group should treat or not treat the grandson of men who committed those crimes, Sarah has already responded that the only treatment criteria for inclusion in the therapy is the welfare of the child. Also, in your hypothetical example, the child is innocent of his grandfather's crimes."

Shaun Sullivan, in contrast to Witkin, was over six feet tall with a full head of gray hair. As he brushed his hair back with his hand, he looked directly at Sarah and said, "I would suggest we discuss this issue of morality and ethics from a more general perspective. I have read Dr. Witkin's book on morality in European history, and I would like to discuss the role of religion in standing against Nazi ideology at that time. What happened to the Jews of Rome occurred not three miles from the Vatican without any direct interference from the pope. Yet, we know from the historical record that many other Italians, including priests, hid and saved Jews in Italy during that period in history.

"In fact, the documentation shows that about eighty percent of the Jews of Italy survived the Nazi Holocaust, a statistic well above the survival rate in other European countries at that time. This was due largely to priests in the countryside and the people of Italy hiding and protecting their fellow Italian Jews. I think that what Dr. Witkin may have been proposing in his suggested topic tonight was that, in Sarah's case, the decision to treat or not to treat a grandchild of a Nazi war criminal who ordered her family's murder is an ethical and moral question, but that morality was never a consideration for the Nazis in 1943. So, it is ethics and adherence to religious beliefs that should be the foundation about how a society treats fellow humans.

"I am not saying that I am defending the Vatican at that time, but from the pope's view, protecting the Vatican from German occupation was a consideration. Also, the pope had to consider that the Germans might arrest all priests and prevent absolution to Catholics in Italy, which is a fundamental aspect of the religion. Was it ethical? Was it in keeping with the basic views of Christianity? Definitely not, but humans are often practical, and beliefs and actions are related to their current circumstances. Sarah has stated that the decision to treat or not to treat a child by her team would be based on the needs of the child without reference to the child's family, past or present. However, I would like to rephrase Dr. Witkin's question for discussion.

"Suppose since only one child can be treated in the third trial, there were two equally deserving patients, but one of them was the grandson of a Nazi war criminal like Herbert Kappler. Sarah, how would you and your group make an ethical or moral decision about which child to treat in the last trial?"

Rubbing her forehead with her hand, Sarah raised her head and in a serious and irritated manner replied, "That is an interesting but a somewhat irrelevant question from my point of view. I have already said that these decisions on treatment during the final trial would be based on the needs of the child patient as well as the availability of a donor in a reasonable time frame. However, I would like to respond to the general question of ethics and morality. In my view, ethics and morality are abstractions and related to one's beliefs within a given culture at a given time in history. From the Nazis' point of view at that time, it was the *ethical* thing to do to murder and steal since both crimes were sanctioned by their society. So, if we had to decide whether or not to treat a child whose grandparent committed crimes, it would not be a factor in our evaluation. The grandson of a war criminal was not involved in those horrible actions committed in the Holocaust, and our decision would not be influenced by who their grandfather was or what he did.

"As I stated before, our personal and medical ethics and values are dictated by what benefits the child and the family. As to your specific example of two equally qualified children, we would have to make a decision based on which child had a more immediate donor match and be more seriously in need of treatment without any consideration of their family background. Additional factors still affecting our choice would include what treatments had been tried previously, as well as whether one child could be maintained on current therapies for the near future. These are both realistic and ethical guidelines without any reference to the child's family, past or present."

"Yes, and you are making my point that your treatment team's decision is based on the ethical rules of your profession," Shaun responded. "Belief in these rules are what humans need to make ethical decisions. I suggest that religion serves this important purpose by providing guidelines or rules for people to behave in ethical ways toward other human beings. While members of a religion may not practice these rules or guidelines, the religion itself does provide the standards for moral behavior. So, even from a purely historical view, religion may have evolved in societies because it raised survival chances for the group by providing rules for social actions to other group members. The Ten Commandments would be an example: Thou shall not kill or steal. All religions studied have similar guidelines about treating others that could be summarized by, 'Do to others as you would have them do to you,' as Jesus stated."

"Look," Sarah broke in, "rules are important, but what is essential is that all societies should teach their members to value all people, especially children, and that every human note can contribute to the symphony of life. This is what my father told me while we were listening to Beethoven on our phonograph. Good music, good thoughts, I guess. Germany and Italy had rules or laws, and yet millions died from bigotry and hate when dictators changed those laws. So when my father told me to do something good for the world, I didn't need rules or laws; I knew what was right and moral. Social rules and laws may be necessary in a society, but believing in the value of all people is essential to defeat evil behavior that Nazis or bigots promote in any country or group."

Debbie shifted in her seat and placed a hand on Sarah's shoulder. "Sarah, I see this topic is very personal and emotional for you," she said. "I think we should end tonight's discussion. I believe everyone here would agree with your view that all societies need both laws to protect citizens as well as the basic underlying belief in the value of every human being. Maybe, as was said, we should only judge people by their behavior, meaning what they say and what they do. In this way, a group can be understood by the behavior it encourages or sanctions in its people. In our Jewish tradition, this is called *mitzvot,* good deeds. We should be judged by our actions."

"Before we adjourn, may I add a comment?" asked Witkin.

Alex said, "Of course, but please make it your final point in tonight's discussion."

Witkin said, "Thank you, I would agree that actions are important in judging behavior. However, I would note that before an act there is a thought or belief. Hitler came to power by indoctrinating Germans to believe in Nazism as a 'political religion' with him as their savior, so to speak. He did this by charismatic speeches with the message that it was the Jews who were responsible for all of Germany's problems. The true believers in Germany marched along without questioning the resulting horrible mass murder of millions. Also, remember Germans were also rewarded for supporting fascism by jobs, money, stolen property, and power.

"So, most unquestioned beliefs, including religious beliefs, are a two-edged sword. On the one hand, fostering positive social actions within a group, and on the other hand, suspicion and hostility toward other groups. The evolution of religious beliefs in all societies helped humans to become more prosocial and less violent toward members of the same group. Yet here we are in the twentieth century still dealing with violence between groups with different beliefs. In the long run, we need to not only punish hostile acts, but also to encourage positive beliefs in childhood about tolerance toward others with different views. So, while the problem of violence, hate and genocide is complex, it seems essential to encourage positive social views and behavior in this life, starting in childhood, and not just punish antisocial behavior.

"So, Shaun, while religion may provide guidelines for ethical behavior, the conflict between violence and positive actions has always existed in human history. I believe that this conflict will always exist in all social groups. The famous German writer Goethe may have said it more poetically when he wrote, *Until philosophy sublime rules, the world in oldest fashion, by hunger moves and passion.* I believe what he meant by philosophy was rational thinking or what today we may call scientific or fact-based thinking as opposed to emotional-based beliefs. I may believe that the Earth moves around the sun, but remember Galileo was put under house arrest by leaders of his religion for stating that in 1632. So, hostile beliefs toward others, just based on faith without facts, can have, and have had, terrible consequences both for individuals and for groups."

Shaun began to reply, but Sarah interrupted and said, "It is getting late, and while this discussion is very interesting, I think we need to pick up on this complex topic at a future dinner. While thought-provoking, I think we have drifted into very theoretical and subjective areas, and as a scientist, I would like to make decisions or recommendations based on evidence not conjecture. The role of religion, now and historically, in controlling human activities is a broad topic, and while important for many scholars, extracting practical applications to current times, other than that people should follow the do unto others rule, which all religions seem to profess, is difficult.

"So, in effect I would agree with Dr. Witkin that one important factor in reducing violence and maybe war and eventually genocide is to educate and encourage children to solve social disagreements by discussion and not attacking each other. How to accomplish that in any society is very difficult, and I think that is what Goethe meant. My final point is that Dr. Witkin's mentioning a German like Goethe, for me, also illustrates the fact that evil is not the sole property of any given country or group. Germany has produced many great and influential scientists, composers, philosophers, physicians, and leaders while also producing men like Hitler, Kappler, and Dannecker. The last two men planned and carried out the roundup and murder in Auschwitz of Roman Jews in October 1943, including my family. As my cousin said, this topic is somewhat emotional for me, but I would like to reiterate that even if we had to treat Kappler's or Dannecker's grandson, our team, and I as their leader, would not hesitate to provide the same treatment we have given to our two previous children. If it is OK with everyone, I would like to end tonight's discussion with that comment."

The group agreed to adjourn for the evening, and they all slowly stood, and, as they left, hugged Sarah and thanked Debbie and Alex for dinner and their hospitality.

When the guests were gone, Sarah sat on the couch and, with her head in her hands, began to quietly sob. Debbie and Alex sat next to her on both sides and warmly embraced her for a few minutes until she stopped.

The three of them did not talk until Sarah said, "I hope I can do what I said and treat any child, even the grandson of a Nazi if that would ever be an issue. But I remember my parents and little brother and anger and sadness affect my thinking, and I doubt my objectivity. Is it just words or will I be able to do what I believe as a physician? I often have doubts, and I hope I never have to face making such a decision."

26

THE TRAIN NOW STOPPED TO REFUEL just north of Vienna in Southern Austria. They had been traveling now for three days and had not eaten since noon the day before. Perhaps because it was in Austria the stop lasted for several hours and, during the delay, the guards opened the boxcar doors and allowed women of the German Red Cross to distribute hot barley soup and water to each passenger. They even let the prisoners empty the latrine buckets before locking them in the freight cars again.

The Levi-Bondi family, while still exhausted like the others, were able to be somewhat refreshed by the soup and water. The meal even gave them some encouragement that maybe the journey was almost over, and they would be resettled soon.

The train was now about 260 miles from Auschwitz.

27

It had been a month since the dinner at Debbie and Alex's apartment. Sarah and her team members spent most of their time reviewing all the data collected on the two previous patients and fine-tuning procedures for the final test patient, who, as yet, had not been selected.

Even though it was New Year's Day, January 1, 1975, Sarah had scheduled the team to meet to discuss the list of potential patients at 2 p.m. in the conference room. Sarah had reviewed the patient application list and had identified four children who met the preliminary criteria and would be presented to the group in the afternoon. She had already decided on one patient herself but wanted input from the other members of the team.

The first chart she reviewed was six-year-old Patricia Jenkins, who lived with her parents and four-year-old sister in Dallas, Texas, and had been referred by the Texas University children's cancer treatment center. Patricia, or Patti as she was called in the application, had been diagnosed at age five with acute leukemia and had not responded to one year of both inpatient and outpatient treatment. Patti's immune system had rejected one bone marrow transplant, and her condition was slowly but steadily declining.

The second child was Jorge Gonzalez, a five-year-old living in Miami, Florida, with his parents and three older siblings. The parents had fled Castro's Cuba and were legal residents now in the so-called Little Havana section of Miami. Jorge had been referred by the child cancer division of Jackson Memorial Hospital and the University of Miami Medical School Department of Pediatrics. Jorge had been diagnosed at age four and initially had responded well to chemotherapy but had relapsed. While the treatment team was searching for a donor, they also referred him to Sarah's team as they had attended a seminar Sarah had presented at the North American Pediatric Association meeting in Jacksonville, Florida, the year before.

The third case, at age ten, was the oldest child referred. His name was Arno Thomas, living with his family in Houston, Texas. Arno had two brothers, both older than him, and was first diagnosed at age seven and a half. His response to treatment was variable with some periods of remission, followed by gradual relapses. Arno was referred to the treatment team by Children's Cancer Hospital at the University of Texas Anderson Pediatric Cancer Center in Houston. Currently, the staff at the Texas pediatric center were screening two possible bone marrow donors and, because of Arno's age, Sarah felt his case should be considered as well.

The final child was Joshua Epstein, the six-year-old son of an Orthodox Jewish couple living in Flatbush, Brooklyn, New York. He had three older sisters. His father was a teacher at the Bronx High School of Science and his mother was a housewife. Joshua had been diagnosed with acute leukemia at age five and initially responded to chemotherapy but, in the last few months, had relapsed and was becoming progressively ill and needed a bone marrow transplant within the year to try to improve his worsening condition. A cousin had recently been identified as a transplant match and the family was referred to the treatment team by his physicians at New York-Presbyterian Hospital-Columbia and Cornell in New York. Sarah felt that while all the cases were a priority, Joshua's case was particularly important as his medical records indicated that without intervention his chance of survival was limited. She also thought that, while Joshua was Jewish, none of the children's religious affiliations would be a factor in the team's decision to select the third and final patient in the trial.

To Sarah, all four patients met the criteria for inclusion in the treatment program, but only one could be accepted as the final trial patient at this time. Sarah knew that if this third case was successfully treated, it would be at least eight to twelve months before the treatment paradigm could be approved for the general population of child leukemia patients since all the data had to be evaluated by the National Institutes of Health. Therefore, the team's decision on which child to accept might be a fatal verdict for the other children not selected.

At 2 p.m., the team members assembled in the conference room.

Sarah entered carrying the four patient charts and her notes on all four children to be considered for the final treatment trial. She began, "I have reviewed these four cases, and I will pass out a detailed summary for all four children so you all can take time to carefully study each case before we begin our selection discussion for which child we will treat. I will mention that I have chosen one child that I believe should be selected as our final case, but I will save that information until after our discussion."

Sarah passed out the case summaries to the team members as well as pencils and yellow notepads. All the team members began reviewing the child protocols and jotting down notes and questions for discussion. As they were working, the room remained totally silent other than the soft hum from the air-conditioning vents above their heads.

Sarah thought that the silence was a symbol of the team perceiving the importance of this moment in their collective research journey. They were nearing the end of the beginning of their hard work, and the outcome of the final trial patient could result in their treatment being accepted for general application to a large number of children or be referred back for more years of testing or even defunded pending major revisions in their protocol.

Two successful patient results would not be enough to gain approval to treat a larger population of ill children. This was not a baseball batting average that the National Institutes of Health would accept, considering the risk for sick pediatric patients. Two out of three might be a great average in baseball, but it would be questionable in a clinical research trial looking for increased funding and a more extensive treatment cohort. Failure in the third trial would mean that further research would have to be completed before receiving funding to expand the patient population. Sarah knew this, as did the entire treatment team. While they understood that two successful patients were of great importance and confirmed their protocol so far, a successful result in the third child would significantly support their treatment approach and methodology. Therefore, selecting a child who had little chance of surviving, either by age, severity of illness, and/or previous treatment failures, could be an important consideration in choosing the final trial patient.

Sarah understood this, but she did not want to influence any team member's decision even though she knew that they understood this fact as well. She wanted to permit all input to the discussion without any initial guidance on her part. She had selected Joshua Epstein as her choice, not because he was Jewish, but because he was in serious risk of not surviving if he was not treated with a bone marrow transplant within the next four months. She also thought that if their techniques could save a very seriously ill child, even though it placed their treatment protocol at risk, versus a patient with a more favorable treatment outlook, it would strengthen the validity of their protocol and increase the chances of continued funding and expanding their treatment to more children. However, even though she had these thoughts about the overall goals of the program, she honestly believed that Joshua was in greatest need of treatment at this time compared to the other three children.

After about forty-five minutes, the team members closed the case folders and looked at Sarah, who sat at the head of the conference table.

Dr. Eve Grover spoke first. "All four children present with significant illness. However, as a hematologist, my opinion is that Arno might be a priority for the reasons that he is ten years old and would be the oldest patient to be treated by our protocol, and he has had variable response to treatment over the course of his illness. If he responds successfully, it will lend great credence to our approach in my view."

Dr. Nolan, the endocrinologist, added, "While that is a valid point, I am thinking that we should select a very difficult case for our third trial, and since Joshua has not responded to previous treatment and has shown signs of deterioration, I would recommend him as our third trial patient. If our procedures are successful with Joshua, it would not only save his life but also provide encouraging information to the granting agency allowing us to move to a larger population of ill children.

"But, on the other hand, if we fail on this final case, our program may possibly lose support, and we would need another one to two years of data collection or at worst be defunded. Nevertheless, my view is that we select him for several reasons. He appears more in need of an immediate transplant, and a bone marrow donor has already been identified and the family is local and can be enrolled in our program fairly quickly. However, I also realize that given his current condition, we may not be successful since he is so ill at this time."

Dr. Tolman promptly said, "Ed, I can agree with your points, but I would add that if we select a case based mainly on the view that it will improve our chances of success, it may not give us the information we need to justify our procedures on all cases, both serious or less involved either by age and/or disease. I think we should be aware of the possibility of not being successful with the final trial patient but not let that influence our decision. Nevertheless, I agree with you that since Joshua is so ill and more in need of immediate intervention, I would concur that he should be selected as our final trial patient."

Ellen Travis, who had usually remained quiet in

previous patient decision-making conferences, and who had a personal interest in the study as she had lost her second child to leukemia fourteen years ago, raised her hand to speak.

"Ellen, you don't have to raise your hand," Sarah said with a kind smile. "We all have the same goal to help ill children, so please tell us your thoughts both as a professional and as a mother who has suffered the loss of a child to this disease."

Ellen returned Sarah's smile and said, "I know I am speaking as a team member but also as a parent who lost a child to leukemia so my comments may be somewhat emotionally affected. Yet my view is that if a child has not responded consistently to previous interventions and is older, like Arno, they should be seriously considered as well. I know this third case is very crucial to future support for our treatment protocol, but I think that we should have confidence in our results so far and that, if this final trial is successful, it will significantly confirm our treatment approach. I also believe that the agency would view a success with Arno as warranting ongoing funding for a larger group of patients. I feel this way also knowing that I lost a ten-year-old to leukemia, which may have influenced my thinking about treating an older child."

The team was silent for several seconds until Sarah said, "Since we have until this Friday to make a final decision, I would like all of us to review the four cases carefully at home and think about our protocol, our hard work, and the future of our treatment approach. We will meet again on Friday at nine a.m. to make the final selection. I do want to state that I agree with Drs. Nolan and Tolman that Joshua is more in need of immediate treatment, so I would be in favor of his selection as our third patient as well. However, while I will take responsibility for the final decision of which patient to include in this third trial, I will certainly consider everyone's final recommendations and suggestions on Friday.

"Since we need to inform the patient's family on Monday, we must make our decision this Friday. So, while we are leaning toward selecting Joshua at this time, please study the cases and think carefully before you make a final recommendation. Also, I know that we are all human and at times it is difficult to put aside our feelings about our work, sick children, and treatment effectiveness, but we should all try to put aside emotions in making our choice of which child to select. Therefore, be aware of your feelings, but try to be as objective as possible in your decision. I will notify everyone if there are any changes to our information before Friday, which is unlikely."

This last statement would prove to be very mistaken.

28

SARAH HAD A RESTLESS NIGHT'S SLEEP and awakened at 6 a.m. the next day after a very disturbing dream. She'd had this nightmare before, and it was always the same scene. She was in a locked, dimly lit, windowless, and crowded room, and she was having difficulty breathing. When she went to the door and screamed, no one answered, and she began to panic as her breathing became more and more difficult. As she fell to the floor of the room, she always woke up in a cold sweat.

She lay awake in bed for a few minutes until she calmed down and wondered what this recurring dream could mean. She had never told anyone about this dream, but she decided that maybe Alex, as a psychologist, might be helpful in analyzing this repetitive nightmare. She made a mental note to talk to him about it in the future.

Finally, she got out of bed, showered, had breakfast,

and was preparing to leave for her office. As she collected her keys, purse, and coat, she was startled by her phone ringing. She wondered who would be calling so early and worried that something might be wrong with Debbie or Alex.

She quickly walked over to the kitchen wall phone and removed the receiver. When she placed it to her ear, a male voice, sounding very official asked, "Is this Dr. Sarah Levi-Bondi?"

Sarah replied, "Yes, who is this?"

"This is Donald Rumsfeld, chief of staff to President Gerald Ford, and he asked me to contact you immediately about a very important matter. I am calling to ask if you could meet with me at our New York embassy mission office today at 1 p.m. near the United Nations building. I will be flying to New York at nine this morning, and I need to speak to you in person about your advice on an important international medical decision in your area of expertise. Will you be able to meet me at that time as a favor to your president?"

Sarah was genuinely shocked at the call and, for a brief second, thought that someone was playing a prank on her. She replied, "Mr. Rumsfeld, could you please tell me what I will be asked about so I can decide if my expertise would help."

Rumsfeld responded emphatically, "No, it is a confidential matter, but I can assure you that it does relate to your area of knowledge, and when I see you in person, I will explain fully."

Sarah said, "I had planned to do some work in my lab today, but since the president feels that my help may be needed, of course I will meet you at the embassy this afternoon."

"Do not worry about transportation," Rumsfeld added. "We will send a limo to pick you up at noon and lunch will be served at the embassy. Thank you for coming with such short notice, but I was informed that you will be making a decision shortly that relates to our meeting. I look forward to meeting you at one." He then abruptly hung up.

Sarah was taken aback by the call and thought about Rumsfeld's last comment. The only decision she and the team were about to make was to determine the selection of the third and final patient in the treatment trial. She felt anxious and somewhat confused as to how Rumsfeld might have acquired this information if this was the reason for his call. She sat down on the kitchen chair and thought about the federal agency funding her research and that the executive branch of government would have access to any information they desired.

This thought interested her and also was somewhat worrisome. She decided, however, to reserve judgment until she found out what was being requested of her by the president of the United States.

29

SARAH WAS DROPPED OFF at the embassy at 12:30 p.m. The limo driver did not speak to her during the thirty-minute drive. He was accompanied by an official-looking man, who sat in the front passenger seat. Sarah thought that the man looked like a soldier in civilian clothes. He spoke to her only twice, once when he opened the rear door for her to get in and when he held the door for her to exit. He escorted her into the embassy without saying another word, and when the elevator reached the top floor, he led her into a large conference room and pointed to a chair next to a large conference table.

As she sat down, Sarah said, "Thank you."

The man nodded and left the room

Sarah waited for about twenty minutes and was about to get up and open the door to see if anyone was outside to ask if the wait would be much longer. As she began to stand, the door opened, and Rumsfeld and two other men entered the room. All three men were dressed in suits and ties, and two of them were carrying briefcases.

Sarah rose to meet them as Rumsfeld approached her and said, "Dr. Levi-Bondi, thank you for meeting with us on such short notice. Let me introduce Dr. Mark Jordan, director of the president's health advisory committee, and John Gottman, assistant director of the State Department."

Both men smiled and nodded to Sarah as they shook her hand.

As Sarah sat back down, both men took seats across from her, and Rumsfeld sat at the head of the table next to Sarah on his right.

Sarah wondered why a representative from the state department was here at the meeting. She could understand a medical doctor and researcher such as Dr. Jordan being at the meeting, as she was aware of his work and publications in medical journals. He was well known in the scientific community and had a very good professional reputation as being an excellent scientist and advocate for medical research funding. She also knew that he had been a member of the committee that reviewed and approved the grant that funded the team's project.

Rumsfeld opened the meeting by saying, "May I call you Sarah?"

"Of course," Sarah replied.

"Please call me Don, and keeping this meeting informal, Mark and John for Dr. Jordan and Mr. Gottman." Rumsfeld continued, "I am sure you are wondering about the timing and urgency of this meeting as well as why Mark and John are present. Let me begin by stating that we are here at the direction of the president of the United States, who feels that what we will discuss today is very important to the interests of our nation. Mark is here because he is quite familiar with your team's clinical work in the last few years, and in fact, he was instrumental in the initial approval of the funding support for the project. John is attending because the decision you make today is directly related to the State Department's role in our government, and he has the full authority of that office today."

Sarah's thoughts moved at lightning speed, and her initial emotional reaction at hearing these words were anxious anticipation and fear. She could not mentally put together why a medical researcher and government official needed to meet so urgently with her. A fleeting thought was that maybe the team had violated some government rule or guideline or some international law in conducting their research. She immediately dismissed this fear-inducing thought, but the anxiety lingered, and she felt a pit in her stomach.

Rumsfeld said, "Let me begin by telling you that I reviewed a synopsis of your work, and I was very impressed with your team's effort and dedication. I also reviewed your personal and professional info, and I understand that what we are going to ask of you may be extremely difficult for you personally. Before you ask any questions, let me have John briefly summarize why our request is so important to our national interests."

John Gottman looked at Sarah across the table and began, "Sarah, what I am going to tell you must never leave this room no matter what you decide. You must agree to that before I continue with a detailed presentation. Can you do that before you know the complete details of our request?"

Sarah looked at the three men and said, "I really feel adrift at this point. How can I agree if I do not know what I am agreeing to keep private?"

John responded, "I know that this request is unusual, but I can assure you that it only concerns your team's research work and not anything personal to you or any team member. I read your grant proposal in which you and the team members had agreed to follow all grant agency rules, which include deferring to the agency in any area requiring confidentiality. While it does involve the treatment protocol the team has developed, it does not affect it in any way. All treatment and research decisions will always be your and your team's responsibility and no one else's, including the granting agency. I have been assured of this by Dr. Jordan, who has been in direct talks with the president. I will also reassure you that we will not ask you to do anything immoral or illegal or in violation of any state or federal laws. So, if we are to continue, we need your agreement in writing for nondisclosure of what is discussed today. I have to add that if you decide not to agree, we will end the meeting now and adjourn at this point."

Sarah was stunned by this request. She thought, *What could be so confidential that I must agree before knowing, and why only me and not members of my team?*

Sarah loved her adopted country and would do anything to serve her nation, but she was also suspicious of any unilateral government directive, as she always believed in informed democratic decisions. Even with these thoughts in mind, she decided she would not jeopardize her team's efforts and the years of research work and treatment to help ill children.

"I will agree even though I have serious doubts about doing so without knowing what I am agreeing to," she replied.

"Thank you, Sarah," Rumsfeld added.

At that point, Gottman took a single sheet of paper from his briefcase and slid it across the table to Sarah and said, "Please read the nondisclosure paragraph and sign on the first signature line on the bottom."

She looked at the sheet and read the paragraph, which stated that she agreed to total confidentiality about today's discussion, with the date and signature lines for her and two witnesses. Rumsfeld handed her a pen, and Sarah signed the document and slid it back to Gottman.

30

Rumsfeld gave Sarah a pleasant smile and said, "Now with that formality out of the way, John will explain in detail why this meeting was scheduled and why it is important to our country. John, please take over and discuss the situation in detail for Sarah."

John opened the folder in front of him and said, "Sarah, please save all of your questions until I finish with the information I will present. Also, as you now know, all of what we will discuss is completely confidential and cannot be repeated outside of this office and that also includes all members of your team and any other personnel in your program. You can tell your team about the nation's request, but not about the position of the father of the child we will discuss today or about the father's role in his government. With that in mind, let me fill you in on several areas you may not be familiar with.

"First, what we will ask of you began as a direct request from Helmut Schmidt, the chancellor of

Germany in a direct call to President Ford. In that call, two weeks ago, Chancellor Schmidt asked our president for a favor regarding an important member of his staff. The staff member is the assistant director of the BND or Germany's Federal Intelligence Service, similar to our CIA. I won't go into detail, but suffice it to say that the CIA and the BND are working together to ensure the safety of both the West German people and our nation. The position that this staff member has in the BND is extremely important as he controls many of the operational clandestine activities in Europe and especially in East Germany and the Soviet bloc.

"Under his direction, our country has been provided with information that is essential to our foreign policy and effectiveness in the Cold War. Without this information, our country would be at great risk both in peace time and if hostilities break out in the world. To use a medical analogy, not having that information would be like operating on a patient wearing a blindfold. I say this to emphasize the critical importance of the information gathered by the BND under the direction of their assistant director and his staff and informants or, in lay terms, spies.

"Now, the son of this man has developed acute leukemia and treatment efforts in Germany have not been successful. Chancellor Schmidt, under the guidance of his medical science advisor, became aware of your team's work and called President Ford. The president assured the chancellor that he would personally assign a team to make the request that this man's son and his parents be flown to the United States and be treated by your team. While Chancellor Schmidt assured the president that if this could not happen it would not affect continued cooperation between the U.S. and Germany in gathering or sharing intelligence information, President Ford felt that, if possible, we should try to help grant this favor to save a child's life. We know that you have one remaining slot open during the grant period, and the president is requesting that this boy be considered for treatment at this time. The young man is nine years old and is an only child and one previous transplant had failed. A bone marrow donor has been identified in Germany, and he will accompany the parents and child to your hospital for treatment.

"We would hope that could occur by next week after your team reviews the medical records, interviews the parents, and prepares for the procedure. This is what we are requesting at this time. Please know that, if you agree, it will be a great service to the United States. If you decide that it cannot be done, I assure you it will have no effect on your grant now or in the future. As you may have noticed, I have not told you the name of this boy for a reason. The boy's name is Hermann Dannecker, the grandson of Theodor Dannecker, the man who rounded up your family in Rome over thirty years ago."

The blood drained from Sarah's face, and for a moment, she thought she might faint from the shock.

Dr. Jordan said, "Sarah, I can see you are very upset. Why don't we take a short break and continue this discussion in a little while?"

Rumsfeld quickly added, "I agree, and during the break, I will have lunch brought to the room."

In a weak voice Sarah said, "I could use a restroom break."

Rumsfeld got up from his chair, went to the door, and spoke to the man sitting outside about ordering lunch and told him to escort Sarah to the restroom at the end of the hall. Sarah noticed that this was the same man who had accompanied her in the limo.

Sarah stood and slowly went to the door and walked with the man to the restroom.

31

SARAH STAYED IN THE RESTROOM for about fifteen minutes. She splashed cold water on her face and, after drying the water with a paper towel, sat on a bench near the door. She slowly calmed down after hearing Dannecker's name and began to think about what these men were requesting of her. Sarah had studied the roundup of her family when she was an undergraduate at college, and she was well informed about what happened in 1943 and the men directly involved in the planning and execution of the action. She knew of Kappler and Dannecker, and of the two, Dannecker was the more ardent Nazi. She had learned that he was a close and trusted associate of Adolf Eichmann and had also directed the *einsatzgruppen,* or killing squads, in Poland and Eastern Europe.

In the reports she had read, it stated that Dannecker was most pleased when he could direct or participate in the killing of Jews. He was also in charge of sending transports of Jews to Auschwitz from Paris and was, in 1943, one of the highest-ranking Nazi officials in charge of the Final Solution. Personally, he was a thief and at one point, in 1942, was ordered back to Berlin because he misused his position to steal confiscated property. Eventually, after his assignment in Italy, he was sent to Hungary where in 1944 over 500,000 Jews were deported to death camps. This was the man whose grandson she was being asked to treat and continue the family line if she and her team were successful.

There was a knock on the restroom door, ripping Sarah away from her thoughts, and as she stood, she felt instantly nauseous.

"I will be out in a minute," she replied through the door.

The man outside said, "Fine. Lunch is in the conference room."

This was one of the few times the man had spoken directly to her, and Sarah wondered if he was there to escort her or monitor her. Sarah stood and pushed the door open as the man rose from his chair, and they walked to the conference room door together.

32

WHEN SARAH ENTERED THE ROOM, Rumsfeld, John, and Mark were already seated, and on the table were several platters of food, including small sandwiches, fruit, and chips. Several pitchers of water, paper plates, and cups were next to the food trays.

Sarah sat in her seat and stared at the food, having a fleeting thought about what refreshments were available to those train passengers in 1943. She was prompted from her trance when Rumsfeld spoke.

"Sarah are you OK?" he asked.

Upon hearing her name, Sarah suddenly felt instant anger for some reason. She replied, "Yes, but for a few minutes I felt shocked and physically ill at hearing what you are asking of me. My team has discussed four possible children for the third trial, and firstly, if I agree to do what you ask, there is a real chance that all four may die. Second, do you know anything about Theodor Dannecker and his role in the Final Solution? If not, you all should do some research and see what this man, assistant to Eichmann, did as a Nazi in the war. I know this may not be relevant to anyone in this room, but to me it is extremely personal and very relevant.

"I am a doctor and for my entire career I dedicated myself to saving the lives of children, not murdering them as he did. Even though it was over thirty years ago, it is like yesterday in my thoughts and feelings, so I think that to do this would be a horrible betrayal to my parents and little brother and all the other doomed passengers on that train in 1943, as well as to all the other victims of the Holocaust. Finally, why can't the child be treated in other hospitals in his country or here in the United States where there are other transplant programs?"

Dr. Jordan said, "Sarah, you raise very important issues in your questions. Let me try to respond to each one in turn. First, a bone marrow transplant was done in Germany, but Hermann's immune system rejected it in two months. Secondly, we are aware of the fact that a child will be affected if Hermann is put next in treatment. I have studied your treatment protocol in detail both in its development, history, and treatment success in the first two children. No other program can offer the same treatment at the present time and therefore your program was the only one chosen. I advised the president of this, and so it is your program or none at this time. According to the German physicians, any delay of even one month would be disastrous for Hermann. I have reviewed his diagnosis and previous treatment, and I fully agree with their recommendations.

"Finally, all of us in this room have reviewed a detailed history of Theodor Dannecker and are well aware of his horrible role in the Final Solution, and especially his role in Rome in 1943. We know how traumatic it is to ask of you to try to save his grandson, but Hermann is an innocent child, who, and including his father and mother, should not be held responsible for the grandfather's actions. In fact, Gunter, his father, was five years old in 1943, and Leni, Hermann's mother, was a child as well. We are empathetic and understand your feelings and what a dilemma this is for you. If there was any other option, we would have never asked this of you."

"Just so you are all aware, my little brother, Mario, was the same age as Gunter, Hermann's father, in 1943," Sarah replied. "My family perished under the direct action of Dannecker, and Mario had no one to save his life. If he had, he would be the same age as Hermann's father is now. I do understand intellectually that Gunter and Hermann are not responsible for the actions of Theodor Dannecker and are therefore innocent. If no other issues were involved, I would not hesitate to treat Hermann. However, the most important issue for me, and I believe my team, is that by selecting Hermann as our next and final patient, it might mean that another child might not survive since it takes six to twelve months to validate the success of the treatment. If I move Hermann to the front of the line for treatment, this presents a great conflict for me and the team members as physicians, since by making that choice, we could be sentencing another child to possibly dying. That we should do this to try to save Hermann Dannecker's life as a favor to the chancellor of Germany and our president to help our nation deal with possible current and future threats from foreign powers. Is that an accurate summation?"

"I believe you are correct in your understanding of the request," Rumsfeld responded.

"If it is OK, I would like to take a short break alone, to think carefully about my decision," Sarah said.

With a glance at John and Mark, Rumsfeld said, "That would be perfectly fine with us," and the other two men nodded in consent.

The three men stood and left the conference room.

33

SARAH SAT ALONE AT THE TABLE staring at the far row of windows. She stood and walked to the other side of the table and looked out the windows. In the distance, she saw the Empire State Building, which always seemed to be not far from her view. Seeing this structure opened a stream of memories. She remembered herself and a little boy sitting by another window and looking at a book about New York City. She recalled him saying that he would be scared to be so high in that building and her reassuring him that she would hold his hand. Sadness and anger swelled in her chest, and she began to weep softly. She sat down on the table, facing the window and took a napkin from the table and wiped her eyes.

Finally, she thought of what her father had told her long ago: to do something good for the world. Maybe saving Hermann Dannecker, if successful, might save hundreds of other sick children and in some strange way be a measure of atonement for his grandfather's evil actions. What would her father have told her to do? What would Debbie or Robert Levy, if he had lived, advise her to do?

She knew what her father would say. The sound of his gentle voice echoed in her mind: *Do what is right, my bambina, my daughter.*

But what is right? Her adopted country is asking her to do something that might benefit millions of citizens at the cost of possibly sacrificing the lives of several children. She felt it was even somewhat ironic that one of these children was an Orthodox Jewish boy, who was in great need of treatment as soon as possible. Would not treating Hermann be an act of revenge, no matter how she rationalized it? Yet could she rise above her anger and act to save this innocent child, knowing what his grandfather did so long ago? And what about the other child who might not survive the year if Hermann went to the front of the line?

This was an agonizing conflict for Sarah, especially that ironically, in her mind, Theodor Dannecker might be indirectly responsible for the death of another Jewish child. If this Jewish boy died, would Theodor Dannecker, in some absurd astonishing way, have killed another Jewish child so many years later? If this happened, it would be because of her decision at this moment in time. She suddenly had the crazy thought that this decision would make her an unwilling accomplice to the evil she had fought all her life.

Looking out of the window at the Empire State Building, she decided what she would do. She stood and walked to the door.

34

WHEN SHE OPENED THE DOOR, the man sitting in the hallway stood, and Sarah asked him to summon the group to continue the meeting. He nodded, turned, and walked down the hall as Sarah went back in the room and sat in her chair.

After several minutes, the three men with Rumsfeld in the lead entered the room, greeted Sarah, and took their seats.

Rumsfeld spoke first, "Sarah, I know that you have thought about our request carefully, and I hope that you have come to a decision. Again, I want to remind you that whatever you have decided will not in any way affect your program, even if we are disappointed in your conclusion. Also, during the break, we discussed how emotional this request is for you and the significant implications it has for your team at this time. As you know, our government would not interfere in any research grant, so the final decision is yours to make.

Are there any other questions or comments you would like to speak to at this point?"

Sarah took a sip of water from the cup in front of her, slowly returned the cup to the table, and said, "I have given your request a lot of thought, and I have reached a tentative decision with very mixed emotions. I need to inform you that my main and only conflict is that to treat Hermann as our third and final patient might likely mean that the other children being considered might suffer or die. Also, you should know that the team has discussed one young boy in particular who, most likely, was to be our third and final trial patient. For your information, the irony is that this young boy is an Orthodox Jewish child and the only son in his family. So, my conflict is even more significant. Namely, to choose the grandson of the Nazi who was instrumental in murdering thousands of Jews, including my family, or trying to save the life of a Jewish child. If I choose to try to save Hermann, will I, in some crazy way, be a historical collaborator with Theodor Dannecker in contributing to the death of another Jewish child, even though I know that this is an irrational thought?

"I hope you all can appreciate how stressful and difficult this is to me. The easiest decision for me to make would be to say no, that we cannot take this risk for this

Jewish boy so we will not treat Hermann at this time. Yet, I think that this might be my anger and wish for revenge that is speaking and not my role as a physician who is trying to save the lives of children. This is a great dilemma for me, as you can understand. So, I have one final question for you all and that is, if I refuse, what will be the negative effects on our country now or in the future?"

Rumsfeld looked at the other men and responded, "Sarah, we certainly understand how this request is a great personal and professional conflict for you. We will not try to influence you in any way since it is your decision. However, I will answer your question. We don't think that there will be any immediate major negative effects on our intelligence services, but if Hermann does die, we all believe that it will greatly affect how his father will function in his role, and he may even depart government service for an extended period of time. So, his network could possibly cease to function effectively and, at least for a while, obtaining accurate information about our enemies would be negatively impacted.

"While this may seem trivial in comparison to the life of a child, it might have deleterious consequences for our country in the future. I assure you that President Ford has considered all the ramifications that we and you have discussed, and that is why he is asking for this favor from you and your team. He is also aware that another child might suffer if Hermann is treated but hopes that this will not be the case. I promise you that if we had any other realistic options at this moment, given the time window, we would have considered it. This is the most rational answer to your question that I can give at this time."

After Rumsfeld spoke, Sarah sat silent for several moments. Internally she was mentally wrestling with her conflict. If she agreed to treat Hermann, Joshua might die. If she refused at this time to treat Hermann, he might die. Either choice would certainly leave her with guilty feelings for the rest of her life and fly in the face of her life's goal of doing good for the world.

Sarah looked at Rumsfeld and said, "I have made a choice, but I would like to discuss this with the team at our meeting tomorrow morning before I inform you of my decision."

Dr. Jordan replied, "From my point of view, I believe that will be OK, but I must underscore the fact that since immediate treatment is being recommended by his physicians in Germany due to his current condition, we must have your answer no later than one o'clock tomorrow afternoon. If your team decides to treat Hermann, the Dannecker family and the donor will fly to the U.S. on Saturday and be available for interviews on Monday morning. So, while we wish we could afford you and the team more time, we are limited by the timeline constraints due to the boy's illness and the recommendations by his treating physicians in Germany."

Rumsfeld added, "I would concur with Mark and also underline the fact that we must be informed of your decision no later than one o'clock tomorrow afternoon. Could you agree to that?"

"Yes," Sarah answered.

At that, they all stood, and Mark and John walked around the table and shook Sarah's hand and left the room.

Rumsfeld turned to Sarah and said, "I want to thank you again for coming to this meeting at such short notice and remind you that you have my card with my private phone number. I will alert my assistant to clear all calls between one and one-fifteen tomorrow except yours, so that you can be assured to reach me immediately with your decision. Whatever you and your team decide, both I and the president want to commend you for your work in helping very ill children. One final comment, please know that the Danneckers are aware of your history and stated that they would understand if you decline.

"If you do decide to treat Hermann, I will inform the president of your decision, and I know he will be extremely grateful. Also, at that point, I will have all of Hermann's medical records and history delivered immediately to your office. If your team at that time has any questions, Dr. Jordan will also respond to any requests, and you also have his phone number. Hermann's team of German doctors will be put on standby on Saturday and Sunday to respond to any phone questions that you or your team may have before you meet with the family on Monday if you decide to treat Hermann." Adding a brief goodbye, Rumsfeld got up from his chair and left the room.

Before the door closed behind him, the escort entered and said, "Doctor, if you are ready, I will take you back to your office or home at this time."

Sarah said, "I would like to go home."

35

On Friday, the 9 a.m. meeting with the team was very emotional and difficult for all members as Sarah reviewed what had happened the day before and her final decision to treat Hermann Dannecker. After angry protests by all team members, emotions calmed, and for the rest of the meeting, a more rational discussion followed. In that discussion, the ethics and reasons not to bump any of the four children they had previously considered for treatment, especially Joshua, was the main theme. Dr. Eve Grover was particularly upset about the government interfering with ongoing medical research and not honoring both medical and human ethical considerations. She insisted that a vote be taken by the whole team, and that if that vote was not in favor of treating Hermann Dannecker before Joshua, Sarah should call Rumsfeld and inform him of the decision immediately.

Other team members also added comments about

being uncomfortable with government meddling and having to agree to such a request at this point in their work.

Sarah acknowledged each objection as valid and discussed each one separately. She agreed with their anger and frustration and reviewed her own thinking before she made a decision. She mentioned her own personal issues in treating the Dannecker child and informed the team about how she mentally struggled with all the issues the team brought up. She knew that the team members were aware of her family's fate in the Holocaust and, if anyone had the right to deny treatment, it certainly fell on her shoulders. She stated that she alone as director would make the final decision even in the face of their well-founded objections.

She related that she wanted to be the only one to take responsibility and not any of the other team members and that, if necessary, she would make the granting agency and the university aware of that fact. She also reminded the team members that they, like her, must put aside any anger or other negative emotions if they met and began treatment of Hermann and his parents. She emphasized the fact that they were all responsible healthcare professionals, and she knew that they all would perform at a high ethical and professional level as they had in treating the previous two children. However, she stated, if anyone on the team felt that they could not do so they should say so now and she would inform Rumsfeld immediately without naming the team member. Before they decided, Sarah asked the team to take one hour to discuss their concerns and reach a final decision without her in the room. She indicated that if the decision was not unanimous in favor of treatment, she would call Rumsfeld to delay beginning the treatment of Hermann Dannecker. She reminded them that she had to call Rumsfeld by 1 p.m. With that, she stood and left for her office.

After Sarah left, Dr. Nolan spoke first, "Eve, I understand your anger and frustration regarding the request from the president, and I fully share some of your feelings. However, it is very important not to think of our own personal emotions at this time. We must only consider our future patients even if we must treat a different child than we had anticipated. We should think of Sarah and what she is going through given her history with the Dannecker grandfather and how it affected her personally. She must have gone through an agonizing process in her thinking before reaching the decision to treat Hermann, and so I trust her totally. We have all worked together for many years, and I know that we are all honest, ethical professionals as well as good people. I, for one, will absolutely back Sarah's decision in this instance, and I would hope all of you would do the same."

After Dr. Nolan spoke, each member of the team looked at each other but remained silent.

Dr. Grover broke the silence, "Edward, I see what you are saying and even though I have strong reservations, I will agree to honor Sarah's choice to treat Hermann. I want to tell everyone in this room that it is an honor to work with this team, and I would never do anything to jeopardize our hard work over the years. I also agree that the only goal is to help sick children, and we all should always be aware of this important purpose. Edward, I thank you for bringing me back to a more mature and realistic approach in making this decision."

Dr. Nolan stood up and asked, "Does anyone here want to object and not treat the Dannecker child?" When no team member spoke or raised their hand, he continued, "If not, when Sarah returns, we will tell her that we will do our best to continue to help our pediatric patients and validate our protocol so more children can be treated. Let's take a ten-minute break to freshen up, and I will tell Sarah our unanimous decision is to agree with her conclusion and meet with the Danneckers on Monday and begin treatment of Hermann. Finally, please note that we began this project as a team, and we will continue as a team toward the goal of helping our patients."

When Sarah rejoined the team in the conference room, each team member hugged her, and a few had tears in their eyes, as did Sarah.

36

On Monday at 7 a.m., the team met in the conference room. All the members had reviewed and discussed Hermann Dannecker's medical history over the weekend and met now to discuss the treatment protocol and review any questions any member had at this point. The Dannecker family was due to arrive for their interview at 9 a.m., and Sarah wanted to make sure that any questions or feelings that might interfere with their objectivity in treating Hermann and working with his parents would be presented and discussed now.

"Does anyone have any questions about this day's interviews or Hermann's past medical history?" Sarah asked.

Ben Heyman, one of the team nurses, asked, "Who will be interviewing the parents? With the previous patients, Sarah, you and Dr. Tolman did the intake interview, and you conducted the postsurgical conference with the parents by yourself. Would you want any of us to participate with you for either meeting?"

Sarah reached over and put her hand on Ben's arm. "Ben, I know you may be concerned about my ability to handle both interviews due to the uniqueness that this situation has for me. I want to thank you and all our team members for your concern. If at any time I feel that my emotions would in any way interfere with my objectivity or my ability to follow our protocol, I would immediately request another team member to take over that responsibility. So, we will all proceed as we have with our previous two families without any changes or reservations."

Dr. Tolman added, "Sarah is a dedicated and responsible physician, so let's proceed to a final review of Hermann's medical history and our protocol for today's interviews and preparation for Wednesday's transplant procedures. The donor, Hermann's father's cousin, is with the family today, and Steve, Ben, and I will review tomorrow's surgical procedures with him while Sarah interviews the parents. Ellen will stay with Hermann and answer any questions he may have and try to make him feel comfortable before he and his parents meet with the team later in the day. If Hermann does not speak English, I am sure the government will supply a translator."

Sarah added, "During our summary meeting after lunch, Dr. Nolan will join us to briefly present his role in reviewing pretreatment and posttreatment blood work and evaluations during their eight-week follow-up stay."

The team reviewed the medical records and protocol procedures and adjourned at 8:30 a.m. to await the arrival of the Dannecker family and the donor cousin, Klaus Schmidt.

37

At 9 a.m., Sarah's office phone beeped, and when she answered, the receptionist said that the Dannecker family had arrived and were in the waiting room. The receptionist also mentioned that three other gentlemen had accompanied the family.

Sarah wondered who the other men were but decided that she would find out soon enough. She took three deep breaths, stood, and walked outside her office and down the hall to meet the family. As she passed the conference room, she leaned inside and told the team that the family had arrived and that she would bring them back to the conference room to make introductions, and the team members would follow the protocol they had discussed previously.

When Sarah opened the waiting room door, the Danneckers and three other men immediately stood almost as if at attention to a superior officer. The Danneckers took a step forward with their arms around a young boy's shoulders. The boy appeared very pale and ill.

Sarah entered the room, approached the young boy, who had a fearful expression, and said, "Hi, I am Dr. Levi-Bondi, and I want to welcome you all to our facility and treatment program. You must be Hermann. I am so happy to meet you."

Sarah knelt to the boy's height and put her hand out. He hesitantly reached out and shook her hand.

Sarah stood and said, "Mr. and Mrs. Dannecker, I am pleased to meet you both, and soon you will meet the rest of our team, who will be involved in treating Hermann. I was informed that you both speak English, but if there is any problem in communication, I can arrange for a translator."

Gunter Dannecker, a man of about five feet, ten inches tall with dark brown hair, brown eyes, and an athletic build, spoke first. "Dr. Levi-Bondi, my wife, Leni, and I want to thank you from the depth of our hearts for seeing us so promptly to provide treatment for our son Hermann."

As he spoke, Sarah noted that his English had a slight German accent but could have passed for Austrian. When he shook her hand, his grasp was firm and confident.

In a somewhat cool manner, Sarah said, "Yes, I understand how important this is for you."

She turned to Mrs. Dannecker, a pretty woman with black hair, and held out her hand, but instead of taking it, Leni Dannecker stepped forward and hugged Sarah and said, "We have heard such wonderful things about your program, and we pray that it will help our son."

Sarah was briefly taken aback by Leni's hug, but quickly regained her composure and said, "Could you introduce me to these other gentlemen?"

A short man who looked about twenty years of age stepped forward and said, "I also speak English very well and my name is Klaus Schmidt, and I am Gunter and Hermann's cousin once removed. I too want to express my thanks for offering your treatment to Hermann, who we all love dearly."

The taller of the other two men immediately stated, "My name is Wayne Arnow, and I am with the State Department and the gentleman next to me is Robert Lasky, an experienced translator who was assigned by our agency to participate if needed."

Sarah shook hands with Arnow and Lasky. Turning to Arnow, she said, "Since our interviews are medically confidential, could Mr. Lasky wait here, and if we need his help, we will ask him to come to the interviews?"

"Of course," Arnow replied, "and I will be here as well if you have any questions or requirements of the State Department."

"Of course, I understand confidentiality," Lasky added. "I would be happy to wait here unless I am needed. During the car ride to the hospital, I spoke with the Danneckers, and their English is excellent, including little Hermann's."

At that, Sarah turned to Hermann and said, "Hermann, I know you have experienced a lot of medical treatment, but your feelings and input will greatly help our team, so now if you and your parents will accompany me to the conference room, I will introduce you to them and explain what our schedule is today."

Hermann smiled and replied, "Thank you for your help."

At that moment, Sarah's cool feeling warmed, and she immediately felt a strong liking for the boy, as she had with all her young patients in the past. Any lingering doubt about treating him was removed by his sincere and simple statement of appreciation. The team's only objective was to help ill children and their families.

38

After the meeting with the treatment team and a brief overview of the treatment process and protocol, Hermann went with Nurse Travis to the children's playroom adjacent to the waiting room. Having been treated warmly by the staff during the conference room discussion, Hermann appeared less anxious.

Mr. Dannecker asked appropriate questions about the treatment process and the eight-week follow-up. Sarah informed them that all this information would be discussed in greater detail when she met with them in her office. When the meeting adjourned, Mr. and Mrs. Dannecker accompanied Sarah to her office.

Sarah sat down behind her desk, and Gunter and Leni sat in the two chairs directly in front of her.

Sarah began by asking, "Do you have any specific questions about the program or follow-up procedures?"

Gunter said, "Dr. Levi-Bondi, before we get into

more detail, may I clear up an issue that is important to us before we review the treatment process?"

Sarah nodded and said, "If you will, please call me Sarah."

Gunter replied, "Thank you for the courtesy, Sarah. Leni and I know of your background and the fate of your family in Italy. Even though I was only five years old at that time, it has always weighed on my mind that it was my father who committed such terrible acts against innocent people. I want to say that is one reason I chose to serve my government to help try to prevent any domestic or foreign dictatorship from controlling Germany ever again."

"Please, you do not have to explain your father's actions," Sarah interrupted, "and be assured that it will have no influence on our treatment of your son."

"Please let me finish," Gunter responded. "This history is very important for us to clarify, especially how it has affected our family over the years. I need to provide you with some details that you may have no way of knowing. What you may not know is that, in 1945, when I was seven years old, my father was captured by the Americans and placed in prison, where he committed suicide by hanging. Before he died, he had sent a letter to my mother telling her to poison me, my younger brother, and herself. She acted on his direction, and she and my little brother died. I was saved by the quick action of a neighbor.

"After, I was raised by relatives, who informed me of what had happened in the war and my father's despicable and evil role in the treatment and murder of civilians, especially Jews. This knowledge has been a weight on me emotionally all my life. After college, I decided that I would dedicate my life to always working to try to make a better world, especially in Germany to never permit such terrible leaders to take over our land again. That is and always will be my professional and personal mission in life. When Hermann developed leukemia, I even had thoughts that this was a punishment from God for his grandfather's actions in the war. I know this was irrational, but that terrible history is always on my conscience.

"Please understand that what happened to your family is a part of my associated guilt. It was Leni who helped me come to grips with these emotions and encouraged me to contribute good things to my nation and in a small way prevent a repeat of those horrible events from ever happening again. I say these things so that you may be aware that Leni and I do not see your agreeing to help Hermann and us as a trivial thing. We see it as a very mature and significant indication of your professionalism and personal dedication to helping sick children. And for that we will be forever grateful, no matter the outcome. So, we thank you and your team in advance, knowing that there is no assurance of a successful result."

Leni immediately added, "Sarah, what Gunter just told you we have discussed many times over the years, and we both agreed that the horrific events in Germany should never happen again. For me personally, you should know that my mother was named Lenore Neumann, and she lived in Vienna, and both she and her husband, my father, were unobservant Jews. My parents stayed in Austria even after the Germans annexed the country in March 1938 because my father, Carl Neumann, could not believe the Nazis would ever systematically deport or murder Jews. He was a famous mathematics professor and well known in his field. He had even consulted with Einstein before the war. He believed that as an intellectual who had also served in World War I, he and my mother would be safe. He was wrong.

"The Austrian government fully participated in the resulting roundup of Jews and Gypsies. My parents were sent to Mauthausen concentration camp in November of 1940 and never returned. I survived because one of my father's colleagues and close friend took me and placed me as a two-year-old in a Catholic orphanage just before my parents were rounded up and sent to the camp. In the years that I lived in the orphanage, I adopted the Catholic faith but never forgot my Jewish heritage, as the nuns were kind and reminded me often about my true parents. After the war, I met Gunter at university in Vienna in 1956 when I turned eighteen, and we fell in love and married the following year. For several years, I could not get pregnant, but in 1966, Hermann was born. So please understand how Gunter and I feel about you and your team's willingness to see and treat our only child at such short notice. We know that other deserving children may have to wait for treatment, and we are deeply grateful for your decision. I echo Gunter in saying that, whatever happens, we will be forever thankful."

Sarah folded her hands together on the desk and said, "What you both just told me has touched me deeply. I know this was difficult for you both to relate, as it is very personal and sensitive, and I assure you that it will be kept confidential unless you give me permission to share it with other team members. While what you have told me is very important in understanding you both, it will not change our dedication to treating your son, whether or not we knew this information. Know this though, we will do everything that our experience and medical expertise permits to treat and hopefully improve Hermann's condition. At the same time, understanding your history and experience helps me to appreciate that you both do not see yourselves as special and therefore meriting being placed in front of other families. So, thank you for your honesty and modesty and putting our decision in a historical and personal perspective."

Sarah, Gunter, and Leni spent about an hour reviewing the treatment schedule and answering questions. Finally, Sarah adjourned the interview and took them to the playroom where they spent a few minutes with Hermann, who was playing a board game with Nurse Travis. After everyone had lunch, a bathroom break, and a brief rest, Sarah, Gunter, Leni, and Hermann went back to Sarah's office so she could talk with Hermann and answer any of his questions in more detail.

In the office, Hermann sat on his father's lap and his first question was, "Where will the surgery for the bone transplant be done, doctor?"

Sarah knew that the boy had undergone a bone marrow transplant in Germany but was impressed with his directness and keen question. She replied, "Hermann, we have a room down the hall where the transplant will be done, and later I will show you and your parents the area and also the recovery room that you and Klaus will be in after the treatment. We also have a suite of rooms in the building next to this building where you and your parents will stay for several weeks as you get well so we can meet often to see how everyone is doing. That sound OK?"

"Yes," he replied. "I am happy we will be staying together. I thought my parents might have to stay at the hotel we were in yesterday. Will they be in the room during the treatment?"

"No, only your cousin Klaus will be in the room, but your parents will see you in the recovery room through a window."

Hermann leaned forward, put his elbows on the desk, and asked, "Oh, when will they be able to be with me?"

"When you wake up and are feeling better, they will be in the recovery room, but, as you know, they will be wearing masks and gowns so no germs can enter the area," Sarah replied.

"OK, I understand. It is like what happened in the hospital in Germany, right?" Hermann asked.

"Yes," Sarah answered.

After Hermann and his parents left her office, Sarah sat in disbelief at what Leni had told her about her parents earlier in the day. The information had sent chills through her body, but she controlled her reaction at the time. What Sarah knew was that in the Jewish religion, a child is seen as a Jew if their mother was Jewish and therefore Hermann was by traditional Jewish law a Jewish child. The fact that Leni had adopted the Catholic religion did not matter in Jewish religious law.

The irony of the situation astonished Sarah. First, Theodor Dannecker, the Nazi killer of Jews, had a Jewish grandson. Second, and perhaps even more ironic, was that Sarah and her team would in effect be treating a Jewish child, even though Joshua, the Orthodox Jewish boy, and the other three children were placed on hold in order to treat Hermann. While Sarah was aware of this surprising fact, she knew that she would never tell the Danneckers or anyone else about this strange and ironic intersection of the past and the present.

39

WHEN SARAH TOOK THE FAMILY back to the waiting room, Wayne Arnow and Robert Lasky were sitting and reading magazines. Klaus Schmidt was also nearby watching a TV near the front door. Standing near the door was the man who had accompanied her in the limo and was with her and Rumsfeld's group in the embassy. She briefly talked to Klaus and Arnow about the plans for Wednesday and requested that Hermann and his family spend Tuesday night in the adjacent apartment. All agreed and thanked her for seeing them and treating Hermann so promptly.

Sarah turned to the man standing and holding the door open as the group began to exit. She addressed him directly, "I have seen you on two occasions now, but I do not know your name or your role. Could you please tell me?"

He smiled and said, "My name is Spencer Ryan, and I am with the Defense Department of the United

States. My role is to make sure that all parties are safe and protected from any problems that might arise during the Danneckers' stay in our country. If you have any issues or requests, you can reach me by contacting Mr. Arnow." At that, he turned and followed the group toward the elevator.

Sarah was not totally surprised at hearing Ryan's role but at the same time was slightly uncomfortable in knowing that a security agent had been assigned to the group.

When she returned to the conference room, the team had assembled to review their assessment of both the Dannecker family and Hermann's and Klaus's surgery on Wednesday.

40

SARAH OPENED THE TEAM MEETING by saying, "First, let me state that my meeting with Mr. and Mrs. Dannecker went well, and I was impressed by their sincere appreciation for being included in our treatment program. I also was surprised by their excellent communication skills in English. This will make our treatment much easier because they will be able to follow our protocol and instructions. Hermann seems like a very nice young man, and he too has excellent skills in the English language. The questions they asked were to the point and on target, and when they arrive for the procedures on Wednesday, we should have no administrative or communication problems. All the consent and information forms will be completed by Tuesday and will be delivered to us by noon on that day. The family will move into the adjacent apartment on Tuesday and be at our medical suite by six-thirty a.m. on Wednesday morning. Any questions or observations from any of you at this time?"

Dr. Grover said, "I will have all of the blood work on Klaus and Hermann analyzed by Tuesday morning, and if there are any issues, we can discuss them at that time. But I don't think that there will be any problems that would delay the surgery on Wednesday since all of the previous blood records are in the files from Germany."

Dr. Tolman added, "Following protocol, Sarah and I and Nurses Morgan and Heyman will be in the surgical suite to perform the procedures, and Nurse Travis will supervise in the recovery room with everyone on call. While we do not anticipate any problems, Dr. Nolan will be available to assist if needed."

"Any opinions on the plan or the Dannecker family from any team member?" Sarah asked.

Ellen Travis replied, "Hermann is a very nice boy, and while he is appropriately anxious, he told me that he hopes that this time the treatment will be successful and that he can be healthy again."

Sarah immediately added, "We all pray for that outcome. I will be here reviewing all of the material on Tuesday, and I would want everyone to get a good day of rest. Wednesday will be somewhat stressful for everyone as will the eight-week follow-up and evaluations of the treatment. I will see you all on Wednesday at six a.m., and please note that if any issues arise in the interim, call me at any time."

The meeting was adjourned, and the team left the conference room. It seemed that each team member appeared somber and in thought as they walked past Sarah.

41

ON WEDNESDAY, SARAH AND THE TEAM met in the conference room at 6 a.m. On Tuesday, she had reviewed the blood work that had been collected from Hermann and Klaus, which confirmed that the donor match was good. In analyzing Hermann's blood, she saw that his red blood cell count was very low and therefore it was medically obvious that the transplant was as urgent as the German physicians had indicated.

The nurses were preparing the surgical suite for the two patients, who were now in the isolation room and being prepped for the procedure. At 6:30 a.m., Sarah adjourned the presurgical meeting, and she and Dr. Tolman went to the surgical suite to join the nursing team and Dr. Warren Hoffman, the anesthesiologist.

When they entered the surgical room, both Hermann and Klaus were on surgical tables side by side, being attended to by the nurses. Dr. Hoffman was seated behind both patients, who already had IV needles in their arms.

Sarah, dressed in a surgical gown and mask as was Dr. Tolman, went to Hermann's side, bent over, and said, "Hermann, you and your cousin will soon be asleep, and when you awake, the surgery will be completed. I know you have experienced this once before in Germany, so it is not totally new to you. You are a brave young man, and all of us wish that this treatment will help you be healthy again. Your parents are in the waiting room and will be with you and Klaus when you both wake up."

Hermann looked at Sarah's eyes above her mask and said, "Thank you, Dr. Sarah."

After explaining the procedure to Klaus, Dr. Hoffman began administering the sedative to put both patients asleep.

As the physicians and nurses began the surgical procedures, Sarah, as in the previous cases, said out loud, "I pray that we may do some good today, and that this child may benefit from our work and live a long life."

42

AFTER THE TWO-AND-A-HALF-HOUR SURGERY, both patients were taken to the adjacent recovery room and monitored as they gradually awoke from the anesthesia.

Klaus woke first, and although somewhat groggy, he asked for some water. He was told by the nurse that he would be given some after he was able to transfer to the bed in the adjacent room and was fully awake. He nodded acknowledgment and closed his eyes.

Hermann was slower to wake, but after a few minutes, he too opened his eyes and, for a brief moment, seemed unaware of his surroundings, but when Ellen walked over and touched his hand, he smiled.

Ellen said, "Hermann, everything went very well, and you and Klaus are doing fine. In a little while, we will move you both next door to the hospital room where you will feel more comfortable, and we can give you some water."

Hermann nodded, smiled, and closed his eyes.

Once Hermann and Klaus were settled in their hospital room and both were alert, Sarah entered the room with Dr. Tolman. Nurses Steve and Ben were monitoring the patients and recording information in their charts.

Sarah said to Hermann, "The procedures went very well, and we think that with medication treatment over the next few weeks, the transplant should be effective in improving your health. We are going to bring your parents in now, and remember they, as we are, will be wearing masks and gowns to prevent any infection as this is a totally germ-free room. I have already informed them of the procedure results, and they were very happy that it went well."

Hermann and Klaus said that they understood, and Sarah motioned to Steve to go summon Mr. and Mrs. Dannecker.

After the parents met with Hermann and Klaus, they went back to the waiting room and were scheduled to meet with Sarah in her office in one hour.

Sarah returned to her office, drank some orange juice, and ate a sweet roll before meeting with the Danneckers. She thought that the procedures went extremely well, and she felt optimistic about the long-term outcome for Hermann if no other problems arose.

Hermann would stay in the hospital for several days to be monitored and then join his parents in the adjacent family apartment, where he would be seen twice weekly for eight weeks. If all went as planned, the family could return to Germany and be followed by his physicians, who would be in contact with Sarah's team on a weekly basis.

43

Sarah and Mr. and Mrs. Dannecker met in her office after lunch.

Sarah began by saying, "As I told you earlier, the procedure went well, and we are expecting no complications for either Hermann or Klaus. As you know, we will be doing twice-weekly blood analyses for eight weeks while you and Hermann stay next door in the apartment. By the way, are the accommodations comfortable?"

Leni responded, "Yes, quite comfortable. In fact, we were impressed that there are three bedrooms, a living room, and two separate toilets."

"Yes, in our planning, we knew a family would have an extended stay, so the apartment was designed to house at least five people," Sarah responded. "As I was saying, we will be seeing Hermann twice weekly for evaluation and medication assessment. As you are aware, we have developed certain new antirejection medications to prevent tissue or bone rejection that has been observed in leukemia treatment in the past. So, it is important to monitor Hermann's response very consistently. If, after eight weeks, he shows no signs of rejection of the transplant, you can return to Germany, where your physicians will continue to monitor his progress, and we will be in touch with them weekly. Our protocol will be sent to them as well as the medication regimen and supply of the drugs. I must emphasize that when you do return to Germany, Hermann must not be exposed to outside germs.

"So, for at least six months, he cannot attend school, and any visitors must wear face masks. All this information is in the folders you have been given, and if you want more copies, let us know and we will supply them before you leave. This will be difficult for Hermann, so a counselor might be helpful for him as well as for you both to help cope with the stress. We have found this to be quite helpful for the children and parents in our two previous patients. Of course, I will always be available to answer any questions you may have. In fact, I would like to schedule a weekly phone call with you both before you return to Germany, if that is convenient."

"Thank you, we would greatly appreciate that, and

we definitely will coordinate our schedules to ensure that it happens," Leni replied.

Brushing back hair on her forehead, Sarah said, "I know that you are both very tired, so let's adjourn today so all of us can get some rest. Hermann will be monitored by the nursing staff for three days, twenty-four hours a day, and I and Dr. Tolman will be seeing him at least twice daily. You can visit with him daily usually after lunch, but you will need to wear the protective masks and gowns until he joins you in the apartment. When he does, we would recommend masks until at least seven days have passed and, of course, no visitors. Any shopping that you may need will be done by our staff and delivered to you as needed. Do you have any other questions at this time?"

Gunter said, "No, and again thank the team for their efforts, and we especially want to thank you and Dr. Tolman for your expertise medically and your dedication to helping children like Hermann."

44

EIGHT WEEKS PASSED, AND HERMANN continued to progress and showed no signs of rejection of the transplant. His red blood count was now close to normal levels, and he reported feeling much better and stronger. He liked playing chess so he and his father would play daily after Gunter returned from the German embassy where he worked while in New York.

As the family was getting ready to return to Germany on Saturday, Sarah scheduled a conference room meeting with them and the team for Friday afternoon. At that meeting, the follow-up procedures and guidelines were reviewed and details about communication with the doctors in Germany and the Danneckers were finalized. A detailed folder with contact numbers, checklists, and a timeline was given to the parents and a copy for the follow-up doctors in Germany.

It was agreed that, if necessary, Sarah or Dr. Nolan would visit Hermann in Germany if his condition deteriorated or did not show ongoing improvement. It was also agreed that Hermann and his parents would return to New York for a follow-up assessment by the team in six months.

As the meeting was adjourned, Mr. and Mrs. Dannecker asked if they could speak to Sarah privately in her office.

When they were seated in Sarah's office, Gunter said, "The last eight weeks have underscored the excellent professional care you and your staff have provided to Hermann and us from the beginning, and both Leni and I are very thankful to you all. I have notified Mr. Arnow, and he has informed your president about how we have been treated and the care that Hermann has received. Mr. Arnow informed me that you might be receiving a call from President Ford in the near future. I wanted you to know that no amount of praise or thanks from him could equal what Leni and I feel about you and your team. We will be forever appreciative, and if you or your team should ever need anything from us or my country, please just call and ask. Even though my responsibilities take much of my time and I often travel a lot, your call will always be my priority. So, if there is ever anything I can do, please do not hesitate to ask."

Sarah said, "Thank you for your offer, and if that need ever arises, I will certainly make that call. If the president does call, I also will assure him that you and Leni have been very cooperative with our procedures and have been a pleasure to work with. We wish you a safe return to Germany and, as you, we pray that Hermann will continue to respond positively to the transplant and hopefully will be cured of his illness. I will talk with him privately before you leave on Saturday to wish him well and praise him for his courage and positive attitude during the treatment."

The three rose from their chairs and, as the Danneckers left, they both hugged Sarah. When they embraced, Sarah felt happy and sad at the same time.

45

On October 22, 1943, the train was about 150 miles from Auschwitz and was now stopped at a rail siding until 3 a.m. the next day. The Levi-Bondis were still sitting on the floor of the boxcar. They had been traveling four days now, and everyone was physically and emotionally defeated and resolved to any fate awaiting them at the camp.

They were told that they would arrive at the resettlement camp early tomorrow morning a little after sunrise. They were also informed that when the train arrived, after a shower, they were to be escorted to their housing units and would be further instructed by camp staff when they left the train. The deboarding would be prompt and organized. If they had any questions, they could ask the staff at the camp. Hearing these instructions gave them a bit of hope that, at last, this ordeal would end.

46

Six months had passed, and Hermann continued to do well, as he showed no signs of rejecting the transplant. The Danneckers and Hermann returned for the six-month follow-up, and all lab studies and clinical observations were positive, showing Hermann to be progressing in good health.

Sarah, Gunter, and Leni met in her office to discuss Hermann's progress and plans for the future follow-up visits.

Seated behind her desk, Sarah said, "All of our clinical and lab data shows that Hermann is doing very well. The blood work shows a normal red cell count, and he certainly looks healthy and has gained almost ten pounds. Let us continue the treatment plan in Germany, and in another six months, complete our final follow-up here. I want to praise you both for following our recommendations so consistently. At this point in the treatment protocol, the long-term outcome looks very promising. I feel fairly confident that, if there are no unseen complications, Hermann could be cured of leukemia in six months."

Gunter and Leni smiled, and Gunter said, "That is wonderful news, and if that comes to pass, we will be forever thankful and in your debt. Also, did you ever receive a call from the president?"

Sarah smiled and replied, "Yes, I did receive a phone call from President Ford several weeks after the transplant procedure, and he thanked me and our team for our treatment and medical expertise. He also said that not only had we helped an ill child, but additionally had contributed to the security of the United States. I thanked the president for his call, and I assured him that I would relay his message to the rest of the team."

Gunter replied, "I am happy that the president kept his word and called you personally."

Sarah said, "You both should know that Hermann was our third and final trial patient in our grant, and if he continues to do well, in six months our team will be applying to the granting agency to expand the treatment to a larger sample of children. If that happens, it will allow the team to treat more pediatric leukemia patients. If successful, our treatment protocol could eventually become the preferred medical care for pediatric patients. This was the long-term goal of the treatment protocol from the onset and, if it comes to fruition, would be a great accomplishment for our team, who have been totally dedicated and worked very hard to develop an effective treatment for childhood leukemia."

Gunter responded, "I want to remind you, that if there was anything I can do to help you and your team with that process, please let me know."

Sarah answered, "Thank you for that offer. I will always keep it in mind."

"Sarah, you know that Leni and I believe that if and when your treatment becomes the standard, you and your team should be considered for the Nobel Prize in Medicine."

Sarah blushed and replied, "That would not seem realistic to me or the team since many researchers before us have made significant contributions that allowed us to develop our current treatment protocol."

Then they all stood up, and Gunter reached over the desk and shook Sarah's hand. Leni walked around the desk and hugged Sarah and whispered in her ear, "Sarah, may God bless you."

47

THE TRAIN ARRIVED IN AUSCHWITZ at 7:00 a.m. on Saturday, the Sabbath, on the 23rd of October 1943. As soon as the train came to a stop, the boxcar doors were opened to a cold, dark, overcast sky and a scene of many German soldiers and men dressed in striped uniforms. The men in stripes began yelling to the people inside to get down quickly, put their suitcases on the platform, and form two lines, one for men and another for women and children. The soldiers spoke in German and broken Italian, and they all carried machine guns, and some had dogs on leashes.

The Levi-Bondi family were the last to leave the car as they waited for all the other people to leave first. When they jumped down to the platform, they were surprised to see so many German soldiers and hear loud shouting and seeing the rough treatment of the train passengers being pushed into two columns of men and women and children.

The first sensation they had was a sweet noxious odor that seemed to be rising from chimneys in buildings about

100 meters to the north. Mr. Levi-Bondi stayed close to his family and did not immediately join the column of men. He hugged them and told them to stay brave and that as soon as they were in the barracks, he would join them to help them settle. He then walked a few feet to join the line of men. After the two columns were formed, a German officer walked down the middle of the lines, shouting to the groups to leave their luggage on the platform, and it would be delivered to them after they were disinfected and showered. Under no circumstances was anyone to take any personal items to the shower rooms under penalty of punishment.

They were to undress in the adjacent dressing area next to the shower room and after being disinfected and showered, they would be escorted to their assigned barrack. Men and women and children would be checked by a doctor on the way to the showers, and some would be moved to the left and some to the right. The two groups were to walk slowly and stay in line. Any deviation would be treated harshly.

When Mr. Levi-Bondi heard these orders, he became very anxious at the thought of being separated from his family and quickly walked back to join them in their column. Immediately, two German soldiers walked toward him and gestured to him to return to the line of men. He shook his head, and they began to yell at him and started to push him with the butt of their machine guns toward the men's column. He fell to the ground and began to say in Italian that he wanted to stay with his family. People began to shout and cry at seeing him being roughly treated. Mrs. Levi-Bondi rushed to him and covered him with her body as he lay on the platform.

A tall German SS officer quickly approached the commotion. As he came close to the German soldiers, they stepped aside and stood at attention. The officer yelled in Italian at the Levi-Bondis that if they did not stand up and follow orders, they would be left here and dealt with after everyone had gone to the showers. His tone was ominous, and Mr. Levi-Bondi understood its implication, and so he slowly stood up and talked to his wife and urged her to rejoin the women's group, and he would see them later after the showers.

However, the officer grabbed his coat and turned Mr. Levi-Bondi to face him. The officer, in a soft tone, asked if he wanted to stay with his family now. He answered that he did if he could. The officer smiled and said it would be fine and shoved him back to their line. The two columns began to slowly walk toward the German doctor in front of each line, who was gesturing right and left as individuals approached him. People noticed that almost all were directed left other than for a few young men.

When the Levi-Bondi family reached the doctor, he gestured left for all of them, including Mr. Levi-Bondi. The group that went left were led by about twelve soldiers surrounding them and marched slowly to a building about 100 meters to the north near the buildings where the chimneys were belching sparks and smoke.

As the group of about 1,000 men, women, and children walked, the German SS captain walked slowly down the middle of the two lines repeating in Italian that when they reached the shower buildings, they were to proceed down the steps, undress, hang their clothing on the racks outside the shower room, and tie their shoes together so they could find both after the shower. Some of the group may have to wait outside near the trees as not all could shower at once. The trees were about 50 meters from the buildings.

As the group approached the trees, the soldiers and the officer divided the column in half, and one group continued toward the shower buildings while the other group stood or sat by the tree line guarded by half of the soldiers. When the group was separated, Mr. and Mrs. Levi-Bondi somehow were placed with the first group separate from the children. Both parents began to shout to the officer that they had been separated from their children. He immediately approached them and told them not to worry; they would be reunited after the showers, and he would make sure that they would be together again, but they had to continue with the first group to shower.

Sarah overheard what was said and hugged little Mario, who was terrified and crying. She waved to her parents and turned to Mario and said, "We will see them soon after the shower, so don't be scared. I will hold your hand."

Mario looked at his sister and took her hand as the first group, including their parents, disappeared down the steps of the building on the left.

About ninety minutes later, Sarah and Mario were walking with about 400 women and children, and a few older men, toward the shower rooms and being told to remember to put their clothes on the hanging racks, and if they needed help, the men in striped clothes would aid them.

Sarah and Mario walked with the group, and Sarah was still holding Mario's hand as they walked down the steps of gas chamber number III at Auschwitz-Birkenau.

Sarah and her little brother Mario, ages eight and five years old, became two of the estimated 1 million children sacrificed on the altar of hate and bigotry. Sarah's life journey had lasted eight years and three months. There never would be a Nobel Prize, and Sarah would never save children from a painful death. These children, including the grandson of the man who executed the arrest and eventual murder of her family, would die because Sarah never lived to fulfill her potential and do something good for the world.

Life is a river of time in which we swim in continually changing events that shape our destiny. In this view, everything that happens to us is, in many ways, beyond our control and related to the time and place of our birth and the context in which we are born. Sarah was born at a time and place where evil lived, and in another time or place, she may have done something good for the world. What could have been?

Epilogue

ON OCTOBER 23, 1991, Debbie and Alex Cohen sat in the back seat of a rental car at the gate to Auschwitz concentration camp in Poland. In the front seat were their hired driver and a guide from the University of Warsaw whom they had engaged to take them on a private tour of the camp. They arrived from New York to visit the site where the Nazis murdered her aunt, uncle, and cousins, Mario and Sarah, on October 23, 1943.

Debbie was now fifty-four years old and having some difficulty getting out of the car. After the guide exited the passenger front door, Alex opened the rear seat door and walked around the back of the car and opened Debbie's door.

He leaned in the car and said, "Honey, I know you are very upset and sad being here, but remember, we came to honor your relatives and say Kaddish for them in remembrance on this the date of their deaths. Please let me help you." He reached in and took her hand as she slowly left the car.

Understanding the emotional intensity of the moment, the guide walked slowly ahead, turned, and waited for the couple to join him while the driver waited in the car.

The guide's name was Maciej Kaminski, and he was an instructor of history and an authority on the Holocaust and the Auschwitz concentration camp. His first name was derived from the Greek and meant gift from God. Maciej had taken many private parties to visit Auschwitz and knew that the experience could be overwhelming, especially for relatives of the victims. He never told any of the visitors that he guided that he was Jewish and that he had lost his entire family at Auschwitz. After the war, which he survived by fighting with Polish partisans as a young teen, he returned to Warsaw, changed his name, and studied to become a historian of World War II and the Holocaust.

With his arm around his wife, Alex walked with Debbie slowly to join the guide, who now turned and walked alongside the railway track leading to the entrance of the camp. As they approached the entrance, they looked up to see a sign in German that stated, ARBEIT MACHT FREI, which meant "work sets you free." It was the same entrance and sign that Sarah, along with her parents and brother, had passed under in 1943, forty-eight years earlier.

Maciej turned to face Alex and Debbie and said, "The Germans were deceptive to the end, so they often used words alone to control the Jews to prevent any riot or rebellious acts before the showers. We now know that this was a great lie, but the Reich was built on lies. The Nazis were masters at verbal deception to gain control since they learned from the top that it is beliefs not facts that control behavior, especially when dealing in politics or with mobs. This sign was on many of the camps, and history tells us that the words originated from a nineteenth-century novel about gamblers and fraudsters who found their way to virtue through work. The first camp to use this sign was at Dachau concentration camp by order of the SS officer Theodor Eicke and eventually copied by Rudolf Höss, commandant of Auschwitz. However, the prisoners here knew where this road from the train platform led and named it 'the street to heaven.'"

As the three walked under the sign, Debbie grabbed her husband's arm and whispered, "I'm scared and nervous, and I have a horrible feeling of dread."

Alex put his arm around his wife's shoulder and

said, "I know, honey, but we came to honor those who perished here and especially your cousins and aunt and uncle. So please try to focus on our mission and have courage. I know you can do this."

Maciej turned, looked at the couple a few steps behind, and said, "At this point, many people I accompany may begin to have very uncomfortable feelings, especially as we get close to the shower rooms and crematoria. If you want to stop for a few minutes, it is OK."

"No," Debbie replied, "I feel ill, but I want to continue."

Alex squeezed her shoulder softly as they continued to walk. A few minutes later, they came to what looked like a caved-in building. Maciej stopped at the periphery, as did Debbie and Alex.

Maciej said, "This is what remains of gas chamber number III, or as the Nazis called it then, the undressing and shower rooms. The Nazis dynamited the building as the camp was being approached by the Russians to try to destroy the evidence of their crimes. It was a futile attempt, as there was no way to mask the horror of murdering thousands of men, women, and children. In 1943, it was operating at full capacity, and it is estimated that more than 10,000 were murdered every twenty-four hours and sent to the ovens nearby in crematorium III. It is possible that your relatives walked down the steps to this chamber in 1943."

Debbie's knees buckled, and she broke into uncontrollable sobs. Alex tenderly held her upright, and he and Maciej stood silently until she regained some control of her emotions.

Looking over at the adjacent chimneys of the crematorium, Alex said, "Honey, I think it will be too devastating for you to go over there. I believe we've seen enough. Let's say our prayer here. OK?"

Wiping away her tears with a crumpled tissue, Debbie said, "No, I want to say our prayer near where the ashes of the victims were scattered. We will never revisit this horrible site, and I feel we must say it now at that holy ground where so many remains were strewn without any ceremony."

Alex sighed heavily. "I understand. Maciej, can we go over there now?" he asked.

The three walked slowly to the area where the remains of the murdered were scattered so many years ago. When they stood near the mound, now covered with grass, Alex removed a small prayer book from his coat pocket and handed it to Debbie. The text was written in both English and Hebrew.

Debbie opened the book, and with Alex and Maciej standing on either side of her, they all read out loud, "*Yitgadal v'yitkadash sh'mei raba . . .*"

When the Jewish prayer for the dead was finished, Debbie said, "My mother always told me that my cousin Sarah was a beautiful and very intelligent girl, and that if she had lived, she would have done something good for people."

The three of them turned and walked slowly back to their car, passing under the camp entrance again with the deceitful sign above their heads. None of them ever looked back.

THE END

End Note

HOW MANY FUTURE SCIENTISTS, DOCTORS, teachers, musicians, builders, mothers, and fathers did the Nazis murder? We will never know. How many of today's children are lost to hate and bigotry and discouragement and will never realize their future and contribute good to the world? We will never know.

Often, when talking about the negative results of human decisions, especially of those in power in any society, people use the phrase "unintended consequences." When it comes to political decisions, I would suggest that it is the "intended consequences" that often result in tragic events like mass murder. Therefore, as Peter Hayes stated in his comprehensive 2017 book *Why? Explaining the Holocaust,* when he is asked how the Holocaust could have been stopped, he gives an exact date and place in the following quote from the book:

The Holocaust was not mysterious and inscrutable; it was the work of humans acting on familiar human weaknesses and motives: wounded pride, fear, self-righteousness, prejudice, and personal ambition being among the most obvious. Once persecution gathered momentum, it was unstoppable without the death of millions of people, the expenditure of vast sums of money, and the near destruction of the European continent. Perhaps no event in history, therefore, better confirms that very difficult warning embedded in a German proverb that captures the meaning I hope readers will take away from this book: Webret den Anfangen, *"beware the beginnings."*

That proverb comes to mind whenever I am asked at public forums when and how I think the Holocaust could have been prevented or stopped. My response is to name a time and place exactly: April 1–5, 1933, in Berlin. April 1 is well known as the date of the Nazi boycott of Jewish-owned shops across Germany. But something else happened on that day, the occupation by a company of Nazi storm troopers of the offices of the National Association of German Industry, headed by Gustav Krupp von Bohlen und Halbach, who also was the leader of the Krupp armaments and steel firm. The thugs made clear their intention to stay and disrupt the association's work until it dismissed all its employees who were Jews or affiliated with other political parties. When Krupp, who was a very powerful man, tried to persuade Hitler to call off his dogs, the Nazi Fuhrer simply declined, explaining that he could not restrain the enthusiasm of people who had been through thick and thin with him as he rose to power. Krupp then gave in, firing every one of whom the Nazis disapproved on April 5 and thus breaking his contracts with each of these people. One of the members of the National Association's governing board, a man named Georg von Muller-Oerlinghausen, wrote a prophetic protest to Krupp eight days later, saying that his actions amounted to capitulation to bullying and that they deprived the organization of all basis for future noncompliance with Nazi demands.

If the German industrialists would not stand up for the contractual legal rights of their own personnel, Muller-Oerlinghausen asked, for whom would they stand up and on what grounds? He was right, and the more powerful the Nazis became, the more irreversibly right he was.

Beware the beginnings.[1]

---

1 Peter Hayes, *Why? Explaining the Holocaust,* 2017, NY: W. W. Norton & Company, 2017, pages 342–343.

Author's Note

PEOPLE OFTEN WONDER ABOUT the meaning of life. One reasonable view is that one valid meaning of life is to help the next generation. In response to the above question, the famous psychologist B. F. Skinner responded by quoting a paragraph from his high school botany textbook about a radish. He said that the story of a radish suggested to him a reasonable place for an individual in a natural scheme of things:

So, the biennial root becomes large and heavy, being a storehouse of nourishing matter, which man and animals are glad to use as food. In it, in the form of starch, sugar, mucilage, and in other nourishing and savory products, the plant (expending nothing in flowers or in show) has laid up the avails of its whole summer's work. For what purpose? This plainly appears when the next season growth begins. Then, fed by this great stock of nourishment, a stem shoots forth rapidly and strongly, divides into branches, bears flowers abundantly, and ripens seeds, almost wholly at the expense of the nourishment accumulated in the root, which is now light empty, and dead; and so is the whole plant by the time the seeds are ripe.[2]

In other words, to Skinner, one meaning of life is to help the next generation without seeking admiration from others, but one's only "adornment" is one's efforts to help children.

In his and Walker Evans's book about poverty in America, published in 1939, *Let Us Now Praise Famous Men,* James Agee wrote, "I believe that every human being is capable . . . of fully realizing his potentialities; that this, his being cheated and choked of it, is infinitely the ghastliest, commonest, and most inclusive of all the crimes of which the human world can accuse itself . . ."[3]

This was written almost 100 years ago during the Great Depression. At the time of this writing most cultures have improved the care and education of children since that time in history. Yet poverty and

---

2 B. F. Skinner, *Particulars of My Life,* NY: Alfred A. Knopf, 1976, page 145.

3 Agee, James and Evans, Walker, *Let Us Now Praise Famous Men,* NY: Houghton Mifflin Company, 1988, page 271.

unequal opportunity still exists for children in many societies, including in the so-called advanced nations. In the twenty-first century, many scholars believe that a nation can be judged by how it treats its children and therefore all nations must pass on the prosocial values of respect, courage, and caring for all humans to its youth. To paraphrase James Agee, what I believe is that in every child born, in any culture, the potential to do something good for the world is born again.

About the Author

R. P. Toister, Ph.D., is a psychologist and former professor of behavioral sciences at the University of Miami School of Medicine Department of Pediatrics. He has been the Director of the Parent Training Program at the Mailman Center for Child Development.

He co-edited the textbook *Medical Applications of the Behavioral Sciences*, a text for medical students. He has published articles in peer-reviewed journals and in parenting magazines, including *Today's Parent* and *South Florida Parenting.*

Dr. Toister has presented numerous professional and parenting workshops and appeared on Educational TV as a host and guest authority, advising parents of children with learning and developmental challenges. He has served as a consultant to the Head Start Program for Miami-Dade County Public Schools.

Made in the USA
Monee, IL
03 February 2023

26979758R00115